"You don't wa........................., ...ar-
tin said.

Shardeen gave him an arrogant little smile.
"Yeah, I do want it," he said.

The lawman was so nervous that he telegraphed when he was going to make his move
by narrowing the corners of his eyes. The glint
of light in his pupils gave way to resignation.
Martin lost the contest even before it began.

The sheriff started for his gun.

The arrogant sneer never left Shardeen's face.
He was snake fast, and he had his pistol out
and cocked before Martin could clear his holster.
When Martin saw how badly he was beaten, he
let go of his pistol and it slid back into the holster. At that moment Shardeen fired, his gun
spitting out a finger of flame six inches long.

"*Bastardo!*" the deputy yelled as he pulled his
own pistol.

Shardeen's gun roared a second time. Ernesto,
like Sheriff Martin, was unable to get off a shot.
As the smoke drifted up to the ceiling Shardeen
stood there, his gun still in hand, the arrogant
smile still on his face.

Ralph Compton

The Alamosa Trail

A Ralph Compton Novel
by Robert Vaughan

A SIGNET BOOK

SIGNET
Published by New American Library, a division of
Penguin Putnam Inc., 375 Hudson Street,
New York, New York 10014, U.S.A.
Penguin Books Ltd, 80 Strand,
London WC2R 0RL, England
Penguin Books Australia Ltd, Ringwood,
Victoria, Australia
Penguin Books Canada Ltd, 10 Alcorn Avenue,
Toronto, Ontario, Canada M4V 3B2
Penguin Books (N.Z.) Ltd, 182–190 Wairau Road,
Auckland 10, New Zealand

Penguin Books Ltd, Registered Offices:
Harmondsworth, Middlesex, England

First published by Signet, an imprint of New American Library,
a division of Penguin Putnam Inc.

First Printing, May 2002
10 9 8 7 6 5 4 3 2 1

Copyright © The Estate of Ralph Compton, 2002
Map copyright © L. A. Hensley

Ⓓ REGISTERED TRADEMARK—MARCA REGISTRADA

Printed in the United States of America

PUBLISHER'S NOTE
This is a work of fiction. Names, characters, places, and incidents either
are the product of the author's imagination or are used fictitiously,
and any resemblance to actual persons, living or dead, business
establishments, events, or locales is entirely coincidental.

BOOKS ARE AVAILABLE AT QUANTITY DISCOUNTS WHEN USED TO PROMOTE
PRODUCTS OR SERVICES. FOR INFORMATION PLEASE WRITE TO PREMIUM
MARKETING DIVISION, PENGUIN PUTNAM INC., 375 HUDSON STREET, NEW YORK,
NEW YORK 10014.

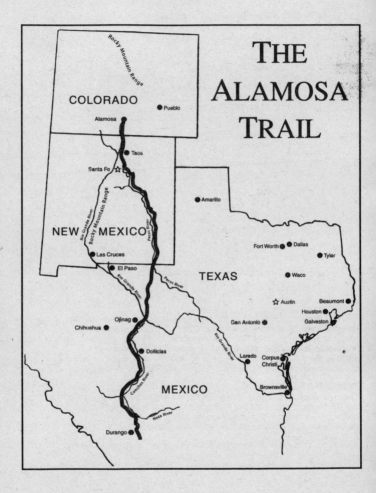

THE
ALAMOSA
TRAIL

COLORADO

Rocky Mountain Range

Alamosa

Pueblo

Taos

Santa Fe ☆

NEW MEXICO

Rocky Mountain Range

Rio Grande River

Pecos River

Las Cruces

El Paso

Amarillo

Fort Worth Dallas

Tyler

Pecos River

TEXAS

Waco

☆ Austin

Beaumont

Houston

Rio Grande River

Ojinag

Chihuahua

Dollicias

San Antonio

Galveston

MEXICO

Conchos River

Laredo

Corpus Christi

Brownsville

Naza River

Durango

Chapter 1

It was a brisk January morning. At cock's crow, Jim Robison came out of the bunkhouse with his ash-blond hair tousled and his blue eyes still filled with sleep. He went into the barn and came back out a moment later leading a team of horses over to a wagon. The horses, not at all happy to be taken from their warm stalls, jerked their heads up and down as Jim began slipping on their harnesses. Vapor clouds billowed from the mouths and nostrils of both horse and man.

Jim was six feet tall, a little larger than the average cowboy. He was older, too, in fact—at thirty-nine, he was the oldest cowboy on the ranch. But being a cowboy was a job he loved, and because he loved it, he never complained about any of it. Neither the blistering heat of

summer nor the bitter cold of winter seemed to
bother him. Hard work suited him, and he actually enjoyed the long, lonely hours of nighthawk
or riding fence line.

"Be nice, horses," Jim told the skittish team.
"Stand still."

As if understanding his words, the horses
calmed down and stood quietly until he had
them hitched to the wagon.

The sun, bloodred and not yet painful to the
eyes, rested just on top of a hundred-foot spire
of rock known as Caleb's Needle, several miles
to the east. Though there were no discernible
clouds in the sky, there was a rather odd haze
over everything. Between Caleb's Needle and
the bunkhouse lay the sixty-five thousand acres
of Trailback Ranch. The borders of Trailback en-
compassed some of the best rangeland in the
country. It was irrigated by the Wahite River, a
stream of water that shimmered in the morning
sun like a twisting strand of molten gold.

The bunkhouse was part of a compound in
the middle of that ranch, which also consisted of
a cookhouse, a smokehouse, a barn and corral,
a granary, a machine shed, and an unpainted
outhouse for the cowboys. A two-story, white-
frame Gothic main house, complete with turrets,
dormers, a big bay window, a screened-in porch,

and a painted outhouse, sat opposite the bunkhouse, and between them was a two-and-a-half-acre garden. In the corral, a windmill pumped water into the trough for the livestock. The cookhouse and kitchen of the main house had their own hand pumps.

Finishing with the team, Jim went into the cookhouse and came back out carrying a sandwich of biscuit and bacon for his trip. Walking over to the wagon, he put the little lunch packet on the seat, then climbed aboard and picked up the reins. That was when he heard someone coming out of the bunkhouse. Looking toward the sound, he saw Cal Norton and his cousin Frankie Ford just heading for breakfast.

"Damn, Jim, you mean you ain't left yet?" Cal asked, still tucking his shirt into his pants.

"I'm leaving right now. I'll be back by noon."

"Ha! That is, if you don't get tangled up with the Dog Woman," Cal said.

"Well, I'll just have to do my best to resist her charms," Jim replied, snapping the reins over the backs of the team.

"I'd like to see the day my cousin had anything to do with the Dog Woman," Frankie said. "Why do you think Mr. Brookline sends him to town instead of one of us?"

Angus Brookline was the manager of Trailback Ranch. The owners were a group of English businessmen, none of whom had ever even been to America. For them, Trailback was just a business proposition.

" 'Cause me 'n' you've not to go out to the north range today?" Cal answered.

"Wrong," Frankie replied. "It's because when Jim goes to town he doesn't get into trouble."

Frankie was right about why Brookline chose Jim to make the supply run. Cal had gotten liquored up his last time in town. Then he picked a fight with the town constable and was thrown in jail. That little episode cost Brookline fifteen dollars, the price of Cal's fine.

By contrast, when Jim was sent, he went straight to the store, picked up the supplies, and came straight back. Impressed by his efficiency, Brookline announced to everyone that from then on only Jim would be allowed to go into town for supplies. But since the other cowboys on the ranch assumed that Jim took no pleasure in the trip, they didn't actually resent the fact that he could go and they couldn't. They had had their fun, and if they were paying the price now, they figured it was worth it.

The trip into town would take about an hour and a half, but Jim didn't mind. Like riding fence, he enjoyed the solitude. Also, the rutted road ran through some of the most spectacular scenery in the country.

As Jim sat on the wagon seat, he could almost feel the weather growing colder. He found that odd, because normally it would get warmer toward the middle of the day, and he had expected it would do so today. In fact, the morning had started warmer than usual so he left his sheepskin coat back in the bunkhouse, choosing to wear a light denim jacket instead.

Now the haze Jim had noticed earlier in the morning was beginning to build into clouds to the west. The high, puffy clouds had started out white, but were now turning gray. He wouldn't be surprised if he didn't encounter a little snow before he got back. He wished now that he had worn his sheepskin coat.

The rutted road abruptly became the main street of the small town of Buffington. There were only nine buildings in the entire town, and Proffer's General Store was nearly as big as the other eight structures combined. That was because Dennis Proffer kept enlarging his establishment.

Starting out with a store, Proffer had built a small addition to house a bar, another for a barbershop, then two rooms out back to provide the only thing Buffington had in the way of a hotel. The result was a rambling, unpainted wooden building that stretched and leaned and bulged and sagged until it looked as if the slightest puff of wind might blow it down.

Proffer was sweeping the porch when Jim stopped the wagon out front. A large balding man with a graying beard, Proffer was wearing an apron that might have been white at one time. As the wagon drew to a stop, Proffer smiled broadly at Jim. A nondescript yellow dog was sleeping on the front porch. The dog was so secure in his surroundings that he did nothing more than open his eyes briefly as Jim arrived.

"Hello, Jim. How are things out at Trailback?"

"Fine, Dennis, just fine," Jim answered. He set the wagon's brake and tied off the reins, then reached into his shirt pocket. "I have a list of things we need."

"Seems to me like you was the one who come for supplies the last time," Proffer said.

"That's right."

Proffer scratched his beard and looked back to the east, as if looking for someone else.

"Yeah, well, the thing is, I was sort of expectin' maybe Cal or one of the other boys would come on this trip."

Jim laughed. "Brookline said he wasn't going

to send them anymore because they got drunk and raised a ruckus last time."

"Ah, it was nothin'," Proffer said with a wave of his hand. "Just a couple of boys havin' a good time is all. What's the harm? And they spent good money with me." He sighed. "Well, never mind. Come on in and I'll start filling the order."

Jim stepped up on the porch, then looked toward the west again. Proffer stopped and looked with him.

"Yeah," Proffer said. "I been lookin' at that too. What with the clouds lookin' like that, and the way the temperature's been droppin' all mornin', I wouldn't be surprised if we didn't get a little snow."

"Hope I can get back before it moves in," Jim said.

Jim leaned down and patted the dog's head, then followed Proffer inside. The interior of the store was dappled by patterns of shadow and light. Some of the light came through the door, but most of it was in the form of gleaming dust motes illuminated by bars of sunbeams stabbing through cracks between the boards.

Proffer's cleaning woman, and part-time whore, was on her hands and knees in the back of the store, using a pail of water and a stiff brush to scrub the floor. She was called the "Dog Woman" by all the cowboys because she had spent three years as a captive of the Cheyenne Dog Soldiers. Her real name was Anna Polla. She looked up at Jim and brushed a strand of pale brown hair back from her forehead. Her eyes were gray and one of them tended to cross, and when she smiled, there was a gap where one tooth had been knocked out by a drunken Indian. Cal had once said of her, "She's so ugly she'd make a train take five miles of dirt road. But she's the only whore within fifty miles, so she's all we got."

"Did you come by yourself?" Dog Woman asked.

"Yes."

"That's too bad. I was hopin' Cal or one of the others woulda come today." Shoving the pail to one side, she got to her feet, revealing that she had tied up her skirt to keep from getting it wet. That action exposed her legs all the way above her knees almost to the bottom line of her bloomers.

"Anna, for God's sake, leave the man alone," Proffer said. "Don't you know he ain't interested in that?"

"I'm just tryin' to get him interested in buyin' me a drink is all," Anna countered.

Jim chuckled, then walked over to put a coin down on the bar. "Give Miss Polla a drink, Dennis."

"And you don't want nothin' for it?" Anna asked.

"Just to see you smile, is all," Jim said.

Anna's mouth spread into a wide broken smile. "You're a real gentleman, you are," she said.

It took no more than fifteen minutes for Jim's order to be filled, and by the time he got back to the wagon, the temperature had fallen several more degrees. His denim jacket was totally inadequate against the sudden chill.

"Jim," Proffer called from the door of his store. "Maybe you better take this." Proffer held out a buffalo robe. "No more'n you got on now an' you're likely to freeze to death before you get home."

"Thanks, Dennis. I'll bring it back next time I come."

Jim wrapped himself in the robe and started back to the ranch. The snow began falling before he reached the edge of town.

Frankie and Cal were in the north canyon looking for straying cattle when the snow started coming down. The flakes were huge, and they were coming down with such intensity that visibility was cut down to no more than ten or twenty feet.

"Will you look at this snow?" Frankie said. "Cal, you ever seen snow like this?"

"Snow is snow," Cal said. He pointed toward a draw. "We'd better check up in there."

"No larger'n that draw is, even if there are cows in there, it couldn't be more than half a dozen or so," Frankie complained. "And the way I look at it, if they've found themselves some shelter from this snow, I say, let 'em keep it."

Cal shook his head. "We can't do that," he said. "If the snow closes up the canyon and traps the cows up here, they'll starve to death."

"Yeah? Well, let me ask you this, Cal. Have you thought about what might happen to *us* if the snow closes up the canyon and traps us? The cows are dumb animals and don't know no better, but we do."

"It's our job," Cal replied, as if that explained everything.

As the men pushed on, the horses kept trying to turn their backs to the driving sleet, so both Frankie and Cal had to dismount and lead their animals. But by now the snow was really beginning to pile up, and they moved on as best they could, plunging into drifts that were sometimes knee-deep, urging their horses on. The men moved to the side of the horses, feeling somewhat guilty about keeping the poor creatures between them and the wind.

"Cal, we need to start back," Frankie said. He had to yell to be heard over the howl of the wind. "Even if we do find any cows in here, there's nothing we can do about them."

"Yeah," Cal answered. "Yeah, all right, we'll start back."

They turned around, then stopped. The snow was falling so hard now that they could barely see, and the ground around them was completely white.

"Which way is back?" Frankie asked.

"That way," Cal said, pointing.

"You sure? Feels more like that way, to me," Frankie said, pointing in a direction that was about forty-five degrees off from where Cal had pointed.

"You think it's there. I think it's here. Let's split the difference and go this way," Cal suggested.

"All right."

The two men started back. For more than an hour they beat their way against the blizzard and the bitter cold.

"Frankie," Cal said. His voice was weak and

thin, and Frankie could barely hear him above the banshee howl of the wind.

"What is it?"

"I ain't goin' to make it," Cal said. He stopped and leaned against the side of his horse, breathing heavily. "You go on without me."

"I ain't goin' anywhere without you," Frankie replied.

"I'm just holdin' you up here," Cal said. "If you stay here with me, you're goin' to freeze to death. I'm tellin' you, go on without me."

"No," Frankie said. "We'll stay here a while until you get your breath back. But I'm not leaving you here."

Jim Robison made it three-quarters of the way back to the ranch before the road became totally impassable. The wagon was no longer a vehicle that achieved its motion by rolling on wheels. Instead, it was an inefficient sled. The team could get through, but the snow was so deep that as the horses pulled, the wagon would push the snow in front, piling it up into a huge, impenetrable wall.

Finally, Jim felt that he had no choice but to abandon the wagon. Unhitching the team, he left the wagon behind. Then, wrapping the buffalo robe around him as best he could, he held on to the tail of one of the horses, and urged them ahead.

Traveling was still difficult for the team, but less arduous than it had been when they were pulling the wagon. And as the horses walked, they cut a path through the snow, which made it somewhat easier for Jim to walk.

"Let's go home, horses," he said. Then, trusting in the horses' ability to find their way back, he hung on to the tail of one of them and followed, step by foot-weary step, moving almost as if in his sleep, as the team plodded on.

Jim had no idea how long it was before he looked around and saw, almost as white shadows in a field of white, the buildings and structures of Trailback Ranch. The horses headed straight for the barn. Jim opened the door and led them inside. Though cold in the barn, it was not quite as frigid as outside, and there was the added advantage of protection from the howling wind and blowing snow.

Jim led the horses to their stalls. Then with hands so cold he could barely feel them, he managed to get their harness off and turn the animals loose in the stall. A few pitchfork tosses of hay, and the team was quite content, already forgetting about the ordeal they had just been through.

Once the horses were secure, Jim braved the howling storm again just long enough to make it to the cookhouse. The cookhouse was toasty warm from the fire that blazed in the kitchen stove. It was so warm, in fact, that when Jim held his hands over the stove, the returning blood circulation caused intense pain.

"Here," the cook said, putting a pan of water down on a table. "Sit there and stick your hands in the water. You don't want to warm them up too fast."

"C-c-coffee," Jim said, stuttering against the numbing cold that still held him.

The cook poured a big mug of coffee and brought it over to him. Jim thanked him with a nod, took a long, bracing, swallow, then looked around. "Where is everyone?" he asked.

"Ever'one's out lookin' for Frankie and Cal," the cook said. "They ain't come back."

Chapter 2

The snow continued for the rest of the day and far into the night. Jim waited in the bunkhouse, but the snow was so heavy and the wind so hard that even the bunkhouse offered only questionable protection against the blizzard. Snow was blowing in through the cracks between the boards and it piled on the floor, melting into puddles of cold water by the little potbellied stove that glowed red from the fire roaring inside. One by one the other hands returned to the bunkhouse so that, by dark, everyone was back but Cal and Frankie.

Angus Brookline spent most of the day trekking between the main house, the cookhouse, and the bunkhouse. He was a good man who was sincerely worried, not only about his livestock, but also about the safety of his men. When he learned that two of his men hadn't returned, he grew frantic.

"You didn't see them anywhere?" Jim asked.

"Sorry, Jim. I know Frankie's your cousin and all, but we never saw hide nor hair of 'em," a man named Tennessee Tuttle said.

"What about the line shacks?" Brookline asked. "Did you check them?"

"Yes, sir, Mr. Brookline. We looked in every one of them," Barry Riggsbee replied.

Tuttle and Riggsbee were two of the hands who had worked on the ranch for nearly as long as Jim had. They were good friends to Jim and to Frankie and Cal, and Jim was sure they had done all they could do to find them. Despite that, he felt as if he should do something himself. He couldn't just sit here in the bunkhouse and wait.

Jim started putting on his heavy sheepskin coat.

"What do you think you're about to do?" Brookline asked.

"I'm going out to look for Frankie and Cal," Jim answered.

"Don't be a fool, Jim. It's dark now. You won't be able to find them in the dark," Tennessee said.

"They'll die if they stay out there all night," Jim said.

"Son, I don't want to sound harsh about this," Brookline said. "But they might already be dead, and if they are, you'll wind up getting yourself killed for no good reason. If they've figured out some way to stay alive this long, chances are they'll be able to survive the night. Wait till morning. It'll be light, and most likely the storm will have broken."

"Mr. Brookline's right, Jim," Barry said. "Ain't no sense in you goin' out there and dyin', too."

Jim thought about it for a moment, then realized that their suggestion was wise. With a sigh of frustration, he shrugged off his coat, then went back to lie down on his bunk. He laced his hands behind his head, and thought of Frankie.

Frankie was his first cousin, the son of his mother's youngest sister. But Jim and Frankie were more like brothers than cousins, because Frankie had come to live with him when he was still a boy. Ironically, given the current snowstorm, it was a blizzard that had brought Frankie and Jim together in the first place.

Frankie was only twelve when his mother and father contracted pneumonia and died in the midst of a blizzard. It being midwinter, Frankie was snowed in and unable to go for help. The ground was too cold to bury them, so Frankie moved them to the barn and wrapped them in a tarpaulin. While the frozen bodies of his parents had waited in the barn for the spring thaw, Frankie spent the time just trying to survive.

When some of the neighbors finally came to call that spring, they were shocked to find the twelve-year-old boy living there alone. He had cut his own firewood, hunted and cooked his own food, and even fought off an attack by a starving, frenzied pack of wolves.

Jim could still remember the day he had gone up by train to get his young cousin. Taking in a twelve-year-old boy was quite a responsibility for a twenty-eight-year-old man, but Jim accepted the job. Frankie could have been trouble after surviving such an ordeal, but he was no trouble at all. Jim quickly became Frankie's hero, and the boy grew to manhood working on a ranch, starting as a cook's assistant, then an errand boy, and finally becoming one of the best hands on the ranch.

As Jim thought about his cousin's history, he grew less worried. Frankie was an exceptionally resourceful young man, and if he had been able to survive an entire winter as a twelve-year-old, then Jim was pretty sure he would survive the night. He didn't know how, but somehow Frankie would make it through. The thought comforted him enough to allow him to go to sleep.

The snow finally stopped during the night, and the next day dawned bright, with a crystal-blue sky. The entire world was covered with a mantle of white, and icicles hung glistening from the roofs of all the buildings. Trees and shrubs were changed into sparkling chandeliers of ice. It was exceptionally beautiful, though the beauty was deceptive because even in the range-land closest to the houses, dark lumps could be seen lying in the snow. The dark lumps, Jim knew, were dead cows.

Every hand on the ranch turned out, saddled his horses, and spread out across the range. Their mission was twofold. One part was to find Frankie and Cal; the other was to make an inventory of the livestock in order for Brookline to be able to determine how badly the herd had suffered. He would then have to report that fact to the absentee owners.

Even though the snow was no longer falling and the wind was quiet, moving around was still difficult. The snow was up to the horses' bellies and it took a terrible exertion for them to move about. The cowboys traveled in pairs, and they took turns riding in front, letting first one horse do all the work of breaking through the snow, then the other.

They were shocked by the devastation they found. Everywhere they looked they saw frozen cows—many more dead cows than live ones. There were hundreds, perhaps even thousands, of motionless black lumps in the snow. It didn't take long for even the newest and most inexperienced cowboy to realize the implications. Trailback Ranch was now a ranch without cattle. And a ranch without cattle needed no cowboys.

Halfway through the day the inventory stopped being an impersonal job for their employer and became a harbinger of their own future. In one night they had lost their livelihood.

Jim, Tennessee, and Barry found Frankie and Cal just before noon. It was Barry who saw the black mound in the snow. They had seen hundreds of such mounds since leaving the bunkhouse this morning, but there was something unusual about this one. Barry pointed to it.

"What do you fellas think that is?" he asked.

"Another dead cow, I suppose," Tennessee replied.

"I don't know," Barry said. "It looks different."

"Those are horses," Jim said.

"Horses? What are horses doing out here?"

"That has to be Frankie and Cal," Jim said. He urged his own horse to gather as much speed as it could in the snow. The other two men did the same, and given the circumstances, they covered the two hundred yards rather quickly.

When they got there, they saw that the horses were dead, but their positions on the ground weren't random. The two horses were lying on the ground, almost perfectly aligned, back to back.

"Look at that. These horses have been shot," Tennessee said, pointing to wounds in the animals' heads.

Jim began scraping away some of the snow. Beneath the snow was a poncho, stretched across the two horses. "Look here," Jim said. "They made themselves a shelter. Frankie! Frankie! Cal! Are you boys all right?"

There was a slight movement under the poncho, the remaining snow slid to one side; then the little piece of rubberized tarpaulin was lifted. Frankie stuck his head up and blinked a few times at the brightness of the sun.

"I never thought I'd see the day when I would say this, but you three boys are about the prettiest sight I've ever seen," Frankie said.

"Frankie, are you all right?"

"Yeah, I'm fine," Frankie said. The smile left his face and he looked back down into the little sheltered area. "But Cal didn't make it."

"Didn't make it?"

"He died during the night," Frankie said.

It took three months before they were able to round up all the cattle. This particular roundup was different from any roundup they had experienced before, however, because this time the cattle they were collecting were dead.

The cowboys tied ropes to the legs of the dead cows, then pulled them to one of several central locations. Once they had them gathered they would pour kerosene on the bodies, then burn them. For several weeks the air smelled of charred flesh, not just on Trailback, but throughout the entire West.

Most of the cowboys knew what was coming long before Angus Brookline told them. They could tell when he brought the table out and set it up for that last payday, that their jobs were over. Normally, there were broad smiles and wisecracks on payday, but not on this day.

As they gathered around the table, Jim looked at these men he had worked with for the last few years. He had worked at several ranches over the years, but none better than Trailback. Even though Brookline was the manager and not the owner, he was a good man to work for. He knew cattle, he knew ranching, and he knew men. He hired only good, honest workers, and treated them well.

Jim looked out at the cowboys who were awaiting their final pay. There were Frankie, of course, and Tennessee and Barry. Standing over by the fence were the only two brothers on the ranch, Hank and Chad Taylor. Standing near the two brothers were Ken Keene, Gene Curry, and Eddie Quick.

As the cowboys stood around waiting to be paid, they talked to each other in low tones, almost as if they were at a funeral. And in a way, Jim thought, they were: the funeral of Trailback Ranch.

As soon as Brookline had the table and his money box in position, he looked out over the outfit.

"Boys," he began. "I don't have to tell you what's comin'. I can see in your faces that you already know. I sent a cablegram to the ranch owners back in England, tellin' them that you boys are the finest outfit I have ever had the pleasure of working with, and if they ever planned to get back into ranchin', they couldn't do any better than to keep you on." Brookline sighed. "But they didn't see it that way. They are not only letting all of you go, but they're letting me go as well. This is the last payday for us all."

"What the hell, Mr. Brookline, why are they letting you go?" Jim asked. "They have to have someone to watch the ranch, don't they?"

"They're sending someone out from New York to take my place," Brookline said. "But he's not comin' out here to watch the ranch— he's comin' out to sell it."

"They must be crazy, selling a spread like this," Chad Taylor said.

"Yes, well, I'm afraid there's nothing we can do about that," Brookline said. Then, for the first time since coming out to set up the pay table, he smiled. "But I'm happy to tell you that I was able to get them to agree to a bonus for you boys, for all the hard work you did in roundin' up the dead cattle and getting rid of 'em. You're all getting ten dollars more this month than you've been getting."

Although the men were saddened by the fact that this would be the last time they would draw any money from Trailback, the twenty-five percent increase in their pay put them back in good spirits, and soon, it was almost like the paydays of old.

Chapter 3

After the final pay off at Trailback, the cowboys scattered in all directions, some going alone, others traveling in pairs or in large groups. Tennessee Tuttle joined Barry Riggsbee, and the two men rode off to New Mexico to look for work around Santa Fe. Jim Robison and his cousin Frankie headed for the ranchland around Amarillo. The largest single group of cowboys to stay together was Hank and Chad Taylor, Ken Keene, Gene Curry, and Eddie Quick.

After three days of riding on the range, they found themselves in the little town of Tarantula. Tarantula was like hundreds of other towns all across the West. Served by a railroad, it had two streets, one parallel to the tracks, the other perpendicular to them. The streets were dusty, filled with horse droppings, and lined with false-fronted buildings. As usual in such towns, the largest and most prosperous-looking buildings were the two saloons.

The boys tied up in front of the first saloon they saw, then went inside. The saloon was crowded, but there was enough room for them to step up to the bar and order a beer.

"We've got to be careful about how many of these we buy," Hank said. "Seein' as how we've got no job, we'd better take care of our money."

"Somethin' will turn up," Eddie said.

"What if it don't?"

"Somethin' will turn up," Eddie said again. "It always does. I'm lucky that way. And as long as you boys are with me, you'll be lucky, too."

"Ha!" Ken said. "If you ain't as full of shit as a Christmas turkey."

"Wait a minute, fellas," Hank said, interrupting the banter. He nodded toward two men who were standing at the other end of the bar. "Listen to what those hombres over there are talkin' about."

"I'm tellin' you, Cannonball is the fastest horse I've ever seen," one of the men was saying. "He can outrun jackrabbits, coyotes, wolves, and any horse that's ever been borned."

"You ain't tellin' me nothin'. I've seen him run," the other man replied. "How much money have you won with that horse now?"

"Near on to a thousand dollars, I reckon, but I can't get nobody to race him anymore."

"Do you blame them? Betting against Cannonball is like a body throwing their money away."

Hank, Ken, Eddie, and Gene looked over at Chad.

"You hear that, Chad?"

"Yeah, I heard it."

"Well, what do you think? You think Thunderbolt can beat him?" Thunderbolt was Chad's horse.

"I don't know," Chad answered. "I've never seen this fella's horse run."

"Come on, Chad. You know Thunderbolt can beat him. You raised that horse from a colt. He's faster than greased lightning."

"And you're the best rider there ever was," Gene said.

"What do you say, Chad? If I can get you a race, will you take him on?"

"We're going to have to risk some money," Chad said.

"With you and Thunderbolt there ain't no risk to it, far as I'm concerned," Eddie said.

"Yeah, I'm with Eddie. I'm willing to kick in my money," Ken said.

"It's all up to you now, little brother," Hank said. "Shall I get us a race?"

Finally, Chad nodded. "Yeah," he said. "Get us a race."

Hank smiled, then turned toward the two conversationalists at the far end of the bar. "Hey, mister!" he called.

"You talking to me?"

"If you're the one with the fast horse, yes, I'm talking to you."

"What can I do for you?"

"What would it take to set up a race?"

"You got a horse you think is pretty good, do you?"

"We do."

"And someone to ride it?"

"My brother here," Hank said, indicating Chad.

The man at the other end of the bar took a look at Chad, saw that he was considerably smaller than the others around him, then laughed.

"We're talking a horse race, mister, not ponies. You sure he can handle a full-grown horse?"

"Better than anyone you've ever seen," Hank

replied. "Now I'll just ask you one more time. What would it take to set up a race?"

"All you have to do is put your money where your mouth is," the owner of Cannonball replied.

Within an hour, word of the impromptu race had spread all over town. Nearly everyone was outside watching, lining both sides of the street. The course was laid out so that the race would start in front of the saloon, go all the way to the far end of the town, then continue on for about another quarter of a mile out of town to a prominent tree at the point where the road made its first turn. The horses would go down as far as the tree, then come back into town, with the finish line being right back where they started, at the saloon. The riders were informed that there would be two men positioned down at the tree to make certain that the riders went far enough. Each rider could pick his own man for that position. Chad chose Ken Keene to represent him.

The boys were so confident that Chad would win that they bet every remaining dollar that they had.

"If Thunderbolt doesn't win, we're going to have to kill and eat him," Hank teased.

Although most of the townspeople were rooting for Cannonball and his owner, Jasper Blake, it turned out that the unbeaten Blake was not a particularly well-liked man. As a result, many in town secretly wanted to see him lose, and a few even bet their heart, rather than their mind. Still, the vast majority of townsfolk didn't think the new horse actually had a chance to win.

The excitement was at fever pitch as the horses were brought to the starting line.

"Hey, sonny!" someone from the crowd shouted at Chad. "Ain't that there horse a little big for you? Sure you wouldn't rather be ridin' somethin' more your own size? Like a goat?"

Some around the heckler laughed, and seeing that he had an audience, the heckler shouted several more taunts toward Chad.

Chad stepped in front of his horse and spoke softly in its ear. Thunderbolt whickered, and Chad laughed.

"That horse tell you something funny, did it?" the heckler shouted, and again he was rewarded with laughter.

"He said it was too bad you weren't in the race," Chad replied.

"Why's that?" the heckler asked.

"Because then there'd be two horses and a jackass in the running," Chad said. This time the crowd laughed at the heckler rather than with him. The heckler sulked off quietly.

Walking back to the saddle, Chad cinched the

stirrups very high and tied them off. Blake looked over at him curiously.

"What are you doin' that for?" Blake asked.

"Just my way of riding," Chad answered. The others looked at the strangely tied stirrups; some chuckled, but many wondered aloud why he had done it and how he would use them.

Blake mounted his horse easily, but Chad had to get a boost up from his brother because the stirrups were so high. The sight of Chad being hoisted onto the horse's back brought more snickers from the townspeople.

The sheriff, who had been selected to start the race, raised his pistol. "Get ready!" he shouted.

Chad put his feet in the stirrups, gripped the sides of the horse with his knees, raised his butt up from the saddle, and leaned over the horse's neck. Everyone soon understood why Chad had adjusted the stirrups as he had. No one had ever seen a rider take such a position before, but many saw immediately that it would give the rider an advantage against the wind.

"Hey, wait a minute," Blake said, when he saw Chad assume the position. The rest of his comment, however, was cut off when the sheriff pulled the trigger.

The gun exploded, and the two riders burst forward. Immediately after the start Blake veered his horse into Chad, nearly knocking Chad's horse down. At first Chad thought the bumping was an accident, but Blake did it a second time, making it clear that it was intentional.

Chad pulled his horse away from Blake, which was what Blake was looking for. Blake used the whip on his horse, and Cannonball shot ahead like a bullet. Within an instant Chad and Thunderbolt were a full-length behind.

They were quite some distance from the crowd now, but Chad could hear them shouting and cheering even over the pounding of hooves.

Blake had several advantages. He had a very good horse, and he knew the course. He suddenly veered, aware of a patch of soft ground. Chad rode right through it, and his horse buckled, then nearly went down before it recovered. Now Blake was two lengths ahead.

They reached the tree at the far end of the course, then started back. Now there was no course advantage, because the last half was merely a repeat of what they had already done. Under Chad's urging, Thunderbolt started to move up with long, rhythmic strides. He was at full speed now, and he easily closed the gap, until they were head to head.

"Back off!" Blake shouted. He reached across

and lashed out at Chad with his riding quirt. Chad, seeing it coming, held his own quirt up and fended him off. Cannonball was a very competitive horse, and when he saw Thunderbolt coming up on him, he increased his own pace, refusing to allow Chad to pass. But Thunderbolt was just as game, and a bit faster, and he passed Cannonball, then opened up the lead wider. By the time he reached the finish line, Thunderbolt was four full-lengths ahead.

For a moment the crowd was stunned. Then a few realized that they had bet on the winner, and they began cheering. Chad let Thunderbolt charge through the line, slowing him gradually, until finally he turned him about and brought him back.

"You cheated me, you son of a bitch!" Blake shouted, jumping down from his horse and starting toward Chad.

"Hold on there, Blake. There wasn't no cheating here," the sheriff said. "He beat you fair and square."

"He cheated!" Blake insisted. "You seen how he fixed his stirrups like that. There ain't nothin' says you can do that."

"Far as I know, there ain't nothin' says you can't, neither," the sheriff replied. " 'Sides which, he done it before the race even started. You coulda put your stirrups up like that, too, iff'n you'd had a mind to."

"Yeah, that's a fact," one of the townspeople said. "We're the ones lost some money on this here race and you don't hear us complainin', do you? You was beat, Blake, fair and square."

"Yeah, well, I don't like it," Blake said, but he turned away and it was obvious that he had no intention of carrying his protest any further.

Chad watched the division of the townspeople, and he could tell by their reactions who had lost money and who had made money on him. He was glad to see, however, that nearly everyone agreed the race had been entertaining to watch, and a fair return for their money, even if they lost. His thoughts were interrupted by a joyous whoop from Hank, who was ambling toward Chad, Eddie and Gene.

"Boys," Hank said, his face split by a huge smile, "we hit it big! We got us almost three hundred dollars here!"

The town rose from the ground ahead of them, hot, dry, dusty, and baking in the sun like a lizard. It was small and flyblown, little more than a wide spot in the trail.

Jim slipped his canteen off the pommel and took a drink. The water was warm and stale, but his lips were swollen and dry. He'd been saving his water, but now he would be able to refill it from the town pump. Also, a drink at the saloon would go a long way toward wetting his raspy tongue.

"I don't know about you, cousin," Frankie said, "but that saloon is one welcome sight."

"It looks pretty good, all right," Jim said. He hooked the canteen back onto the saddle pommel, then urged his horse forward with the barest suggestion of a squeeze from his knees. As the two rode down the street, the hoofbeats sounded hollow on the sun-baked surface, and little puffs of dust drifted up to hang suspended behind them as if reluctant to return to the hot, hard ground.

Jim rode into the clapboard town slowly, sizing it up as he did so. It was a one-street town with a few shacks made of whip-sawed lumber, the unpainted wood splitting and turning gray, the houses leaning as if bent by the wind. There was no railroad serving the town, so no signs of the outside world greeted them. It was a self-contained little community, inbred and festering.

They examined the buildings as they passed them by. There was a rooming house, a livery stable with a smithy's shop to one side, and a general store with a sign that said DRUGS, MEATS, GOODS on its high false front. Next to the general store was the saloon. It was the only painted building in town.

The two men rode up to the hitch-rail in front of the saloon, dismounted, and patted their clothes, sending up plumes of dust that settled again on the cloth like a fly swarm. A small boy sucking on a red-and-white peppermint stick peered at them from the general store's dust-glazed front window. A woman's hand came from the shadows of the store to snatch the boy away.

The woman who pulled the boy away might have been pretty at one point in her life, but she looked old before her time now. The sun and wind and the backbreaking life had made the twenty-six-year-old look forty.

"Who are they, Mama?" the boy asked.

"No doubt they are out-of-work cowboys," the woman replied. "Ever since that big freeze last winter the country is full of them. Now come away from the window. Whoever they are is none of our business."

Unaware that they had been the subject of conversation, Jim and Frankie looked up and down the street. A few buildings away, a door slammed and an isinglass shade came down on the upstairs window of the boardinghouse. A sign creaked in the wind and flies buzzed loudly around a nearby pile of horse manure.

These sounds were magnified because, despite the conversation in the general store, the street itself was dead silent. Jim and Frankie heard no human voices, yet they knew there were people around, for there were horses tied here and there, including several in front of the saloon.

Boot heels banged on the boardwalk in front of the saloon and a shadow fell across Jim and Frankie. The two men looked up to see three men standing in front of them. The men were rough-looking, with sweeping mustaches and beady eyes. They stood across the walk, barring the way into the saloon.

"You boys get back on your horses and just keep on riding," the one in the middle said. He was the ugliest and meanest-looking of the three, probably because he had a drooping eyelid. "We've about had our fill of out-of-work cowboys."

"We'll be on our way soon as we get water, a little food, and a couple of beers," Jim said.

"You'll be on your way now," Droopy-eye said. He was wearing a duster, and he pulled it back to one side to expose a long-barrel pistol sheathed in a holster that was tied halfway down his leg. The other two men made the same threatening motion.

"Mister, I hope you don't work for the town's welcoming committee," Jim said.

"This here ain't no joke," Droopy-eye replied.

"Didn't think it was," Jim said. "At least, I wasn't finding it funny. Now step aside. My cousin and I are going into the saloon."

Droopy-eye shook his head. "I don't think so," he said.

"Frankie, if they start something, you take that muley-looking son of a bitch on the right. I'll kill the loudmouth with the lazy eye and that ugly bastard one on the left."

"All right, cousin," Frankie replied, easily. The exchange was quiet and matter-of-fact, but spoken with the finality of someone who intended to do what he said.

"You crazy, mister?" Droopy-eye asked. "There are three of us."

"Just thirsty," Jim replied. "Now in the next moment I'm goin' to be killin' or drinkin'. It's your call."

For a moment, Jim thought Droopy-eye was going to take the challenge. Then he saw the fight leave his eyes, and the man shrugged.

"After you two have our food and drink, get on out of town," he said. "I meant it when I said we don't want your kind around." He looked at his two partners, who also seemed to have lost the spirit when they saw their leader back down. "Come on," he said.

With their way no longer barred, Jim and Frankie went into the saloon and headed straight for the bar, where they ordered a beer.

"Barkeep, those beers are on me," a man said from the other end of the bar, "and as many more as they can drink."

"Yes, sir," the bartender said, drawing two foaming beers, then setting the mugs in front of Jim and Frankie.

"Thanks," Jim said, holding the beer up. Then, recognizing his benefactor, he smiled. "Clay Allison."

"Do I know you?" Allison asked.

"No, not exactly. But I know who you are."

Allison nodded. "Yes, too many people do, I'm afraid. Listen, I saw the way you two boys handled yourselves out there, and I was impressed by it. So impressed that I'd like to offer you a job, if you're interested."

Jim took a long, Adam's-apple-bobbing swallow of his beer, then wiped the foam from his lips with the back of his hand before he answered.

"It just so happens we are out of work right now," Jim said. "We're interested."

"It's a pretty big job and it's going to take more than the two of you. It's in El Paso. You think you could round up an outfit?"

"Oh, yes," Jim replied. "I know just where to go."

Chapter 4

After learning of the job opportunity, Jim sent telegrams to several of their friends, asking them to meet Frankie and him in El Paso. Without waiting for any replies, they set out for El Paso themselves, aiming to reach the border town within two more days.

"You sure there's really work for us, Jim?" Frankie asked, pulling his horse up to ride abreast of his cousin.

"I'm sure."

"How do you know?"

"Say what you want about Clay Allison, but I believe him to be a man of his word. If he said he has work for us, he has work for us."

"I hope so. After we sent telegrams to everyone asking them to meet us, I'd hate to have to face 'em and tell 'em it was all a mistake."

"Listen, he gave us twenty-five dollars apiece to meet him there, didn't he? You think he would have done that if he didn't have anything for us? There's no way he would just give that money away."

"Yeah, I guess you're right. Now our only problem is if the telegrams reached the people we sent them to. And if they'll actually come, once they get the wires."

"I figured we owe the boys who rode in the Trailback outfit with us the first chance," Jim said. "But if nobody shows up, we'll hire some men in El Paso. You got any idea how many out-of-work cowboys would kill for this job?"

The two cousins continued to ride through land that was red, brown, and open. They were in southwest Texas, where there were few houses, fields, or even ranches to break up the vistas. The horizons were studded with red mesas and purple cliff walls, and in the distance they saw blue mountains. When night came, the stars and moon shed so much light that, though everything was in shades of silver and black, they could see almost as clearly as at midday.

The next morning they found themselves in the small village of Sierra Blanco. Hot and dusty, the town was little more than a two-block-long main street with flyblown adobe buildings on either side. The cousins stopped to stable their horses; then they crossed the street to the saloon for food and a few drinks.

Lunch was steak and beans liberally seasoned with hot peppers. They washed the meal down with mugs of beer.

"Those beans'll set you afire," Frankie warned. "But damn me if they aren't about the tastiest things I've put in my mouth in quite a while."

"You ate them so fast, how would you know what they taste like?" Jim teased.

Whereas Frankie was already finished with his meal, Jim was less than halfway through.

"I wanted to get the eating out of the way so I could get on to the more important things," Frankie said. He smiled at one of the bar girls, and she caught his smile and returned it.

"Yes, I see what you consider more important."

"Oh, now, look at that smile, would you, cousin? She sure is somewhat more winsome than Dog Woman."

"Anyone is more winsome than Dog Woman."

"I do believe that little girl is falling in love with me," Frankie insisted.

"She's in love within anyone who has two dollars to take her upstairs," Jim replied.

"Well, then, doesn't this work out well? It just so happens that I have two dollars." Frankie stood up. "I won't be long."

"You never are," Jim replied with a chuckle.

Shortly after Frankie went upstairs with the girl, a man came into the saloon and stepped up to the bar. He moved down to the far end where he could see the whole saloon, and he examined everyone through dark, shifty eyes. He was small, wiry, and dark, with a narrow nose, thin lips, and a scar, like a purple lightning flash that started just above his left eye, hooked through it leaving a puffy mass of flesh, then came down his cheek to hook up under the corner of his mouth. He used his left hand to hold his glass while his right stayed down beside the handle of his Colt .44. The pistol, Jim noticed, was being worn in such a way as to allow for a quick draw.

Of all the customers in the saloon, only Jim had actually noticed the man, and as he continued to eat, he studied the small dark man carefully. Jim knew that this man, whomever he was, was about to kill someone. He knew it as clearly as if the man had been dressed in a black robe, carrying a scythe, and wearing a death's-head.

The beaded strings that hung over the front

door clacked loudly as two men came into the saloon. The new arrivals were wearing badges, and they stood just inside the entrance for a moment, peering around the room. One of them had eyes to match his gray hair and mustache, and wore a sheriff's star. His deputy was much younger, and from the man's dark hair and eyes, Jim guessed he might have been Mexican.

The two lawmen studied the room until their gaze found the beady-eyed man at the bar. Their muscles stiffened, and when Jim looked toward the small dark man, he realized this was what he had been waiting for.

"Mister, would your name be Will Shardeen?" the sheriff asked.

"What if it is?"

"You got a lot of gall, comin' into my town."

"I ain't got no argument with you, Sheriff."

"Don't matter whether you have or not. I've got a whole drawerful of dodgers on you, so I'm goin' to have to put you under arrest. You goin' to come easy, or hard?"

"I ain't comin' at all," Shardeen answered.

"Oh, you're comin', all right," the sheriff insisted.

"I'd advise you to back off, Sheriff," Shardeen said. "Like I told you, I ain't got no argument with you, unless you push it."

Shardeen's voice was high, thin, and grating. In a world without weapons he might have been a pathetic figure among men, but his long, thin fingers, delicate hands, and small, wiry body were perfectly suited for his occupation as a gunman. "Now why don't you just back on out the door before this goes any further?"

The sheriff shook his head. "I can't do that, Shardeen," he said. "I can't just walk away from this. This is the way I make my livin'."

"All I can say is, it's a hell of a way to make a livin'," Shardeen replied.

Using his left hand, Shardeen put his drink down, then stepped away from the bar. The sheriff's deputy stepped several feet to one side while still facing Shardeen. He bent his knees slightly and held his hand in readiness over his own pistol.

"Well, let's do it, Sheriff," Shardeen said.

"You don't want this, Shardeen."

Shardeen smiled, an arrogant little smile. "Yeah, I do want it," he said.

Jim saw the sheriff lick his lips nervously, then look around the room.

"Any of you fellas willin' to sign on as my deputy?" he asked.

No one volunteered. In fact, several men who considered themselves too close to any possible action got up and moved away. Only Jim remained at his table.

"You?" the sheriff called hopefully to Jim. "You want to sign on?"

"Sorry, Sheriff. This just isn't any of my business," Jim replied.

"Yeah," the sheriff said. Again, he licked his lips. "Can't say I blame you."

"Looks like you're on your own, Sheriff," Shardeen said. "It's still not too late for you to walk away."

"No, I . . . I can't do that," the sheriff said. He held his hand out toward his deputy. "Ernesto, you better stay out of this. Your wife just had a baby."

"I'm no' goin' let you face this hombre alone, Senor Martin," the deputy said. His swarthy face was bathed with sweat, though it wasn't that hot right now.

Jim turned his attention back to Sheriff Martin. The lawman was so nervous that he telegraphed when he was going to make his move by the narrowing of the corners of his eyes, the glint of light in his pupils, then the resignation. Martin lost the contest even before it began.

The sheriff started for his gun.

The arrogant smile never left Shardeen's face. He was snake fast. He had his pistol out and cocked, before Martin could clear his holster. When Martin saw how badly beaten he was, he let go of his pistol, and it slid back into the holster. At that moment Shardeen fired, his gun spitting a finger of flame six inches long.

"Bastardo!" the deputy yelled as he pulled his own gun.

Shardeen's gun roared a second time. Ernesto, like Sheriff Martin, was unable to get off a shot. A large cloud of smoke billowed up from Shardeen's gun. As the smoke drifted to the ceiling Shardeen stood there, the smoking gun in his hand, the arrogant smile still on his face. The sheriff and his deputy were dead on the floor.

Jim heard footsteps running upstairs, and when he saw Shardeen whip his gun around, Jim drew his gun behind Shardeen's back. Shardeen heard the deadly click of sear on cylinder as the hammer came back on Jim's gun. He looked around to see that Jim had the drop on him.

"Mister, you already dealt yourself out of this. Have you gone crazy?" Shardeen asked.

"No, I don't think so," Jim answered. "But that's my cousin up there. I wouldn't take it too kindly to see you shoot him."

"You shoulda stayed out of it," Shardeen said in a grating voice. From the look on his face, it was obvious that Shardeen was thinking about calling Jim's bluff.

Jim smiled at Shardeen, an icy smile that told the gunman he wasn't afraid.

"You're thinking about trying me, aren't you?" Jim asked in a voice that was calm as if he were calling a bluff in a poker game. "Well, go ahead. You're pretty fast. You might beat me."

"Why don't you put your gun away?" Shardeen asked. "We'll do this fair and square."

"No, I have a better idea. I think I'll just kill you and get it over with."

"No!" Shardeen shouted in sudden fear. It was the kind of fear he instilled in others and everyone in the saloon watched in morbid fascination as the drama played out before them.

"Get out of here," Jim said.

Shardeen's face curled into a vicious sneer as he slipped his pistol back into its holster.

"We may run into each other again," Shardeen warned. "When the odds are more even."

"Could be," Jim admitted.

"I'll be lookin' forward to it," Shardeen said. Backing carefully across the floor, he put his hand behind him, feeling for the beaded strings. Once he found them, he slipped through them, then was gone.

*   *   *

Ten miles out of Santa Fe, a heavy, booming thunder rolled over the gray veils of rain and the ominous black clouds that crowded the hills. Though it had not yet reached them, the storm was moving quickly, and Barry Riggsbee and Tennessee Tuttle took ponchos from their saddlebags, shook them out, then slipped them on to be prepared for the impending downpour.

Barry was about five foot eight, ash-blond, young in years, but with the hard face and the seasoned blue eyes of someone who had seen more than his share of hard times. Tennessee was six foot one, with broad shoulders and dark hair. Having found no work in Santa Fe, the two were about to leave for Texas when a telegram from Jim Robison arrived telling them of some job riding for Clay Allison.

"Tennessee, we need to find us some place to get!" Barry called.

"Take a look over there," Tennessee called back. "Looks like a line shack."

"Looks deserted, though."

"All the better," Tennessee insisted.

The line shack was a good two miles away and the rain broke about halfway there. They prodded the horses into a trot and covered the last mile in short order. A lean-to extended from the side of the shack, and the two cowboys put their horses under the makeshift shelter before they went inside.

The door was padlocked from the outside, proof, if proof was needed, that the shack was empty. Tennessee jerked on the padlock to make certain that it was really locked.

It was.

"So what do we do now?" Barry asked.

Tennessee thought for no more than a moment, then he rammed his shoulder into the door. With a wrenching sound, the hasp tore loose.

"Hated to do that," Tennessee said. "But it serves 'em right for being so mean as to lock a place like this. They had to know that from time to time someone might need it for shelter."

"That's probably why they locked it," Barry said. "To keep people like us out."

"Yeah? Well, then I'm glad I broke in." With Tennessee leading the way, the two men stepped inside.

A dim, watery light filtered through dirty windows, barely pushing back the shadows. It was cold and damp and the air of the little deserted shack was redolent with the sour odor of being closed up for a while. But the stale smell of woodsmoke from fires long extinguished still lingered.

"Wonder if there's anything in the possibles drawer?" Barry asked, as he started rifling through the cabinet.

"You know there ain't goin' to be," Tennessee said. "Whoever wintered here done just what we done. They stayed until the last drop of coffee was drunk and the last bean was et."

"Ha! They left some matches!" Barry said, triumphantly holding up a box. "Leastwise, we can get us a fire goin'."

Half an hour later, with the rain coming down hard outside and a wood fire snapping in the little potbellied stove inside, Barry Riggsbee and Tennessee Tuttle drank the last of their coffee and chewed on a piece of jerky.

"Well, now, all things told, I'd say we're livin' in high cotton," Tennessee said as he pulled his boots off and held his feet toward the stove. "We got a roof to keep the rain off, and a fire to drive out the cold."

"A beer would be nice," Barry said.

Tennessee snorted what might have been a laugh. "A beer?"

"Yeah. I mean, let's keep this in perspective. Being inside by a warm fire is nicer than being outside in the rain. But it lacks a hell of a lot in being tall cotton."

"Damn, you'd bitch if you got hung with a new rope," Tennessee said with a laugh.

Barry was quiet for a moment, then he asked, very solemnly, "Tennessee, you ever see a man get hung?"

"Uh, no, not really," Tennessee answered. "I was in a crowd once when they hung someone, but he was on the other side of the fence from me so I didn't really get to see anything. How 'bout you?"

"I saw a man lynched once," Barry answered. "It wasn't a pretty sight." Unconsciously, he pulled his collar away from his neck. He cleared his throat, then changed subjects. "I bet it's two more days before we make El Paso. If our food lasts that long."

"We don't have to worry none about our food lastin'. More'n likely I'll still be chewin' on this same piece of jerky," Tennessee said, holding up the piece of withered meat. Both men laughed.

"Wonder what ranch this is?" Barry asked as he looked around the little cabin.

"Not much tellin'. 'Bout the only thing for sure it, it prob'ly had as big a cow die-up as any of the other ranches did. Else there'd still be cowboys here," Tennessee replied.

"I'll say this for 'em—the cowboys that worked here had a good place to winter in. I've seen lot worse line shacks."

"That's true. We've wintered in worse ourselves," Tennessee said.

Barry let his eyes sweep slowly around the little cabin.

"Hey, there's a newspaper," he said, pointing to a shelf over one of the bunks.

"It's prob'ly old."

"What difference does that make? I haven't even seen a newspaper in a month of Sundays. No matter how old it is it'll be news to me." Barry retrieved the paper. "It's dated March third, 1886. What's today's date?"

"Damn if I know," Tennessee answered. "I think it's 1886, though."

"From the cold rain, I'd make it late March or early April," Barry said. "So the paper isn't all that old." He read for a moment, then whistled softly. "Well, imagine that."

"What?"

"Out in California they're loading oranges onto trains and sending them all the way to New York to sell."

"Yeah? We live in amazin' times, don't we?" Tennessee replied.

"I reckon we do."

"What else does it say?"

"There's a story in here about the big snowstorm. They're callin' it the 'Blizzard of 1886.'"

"What's it say?"

"It' started on January sixth, and they're calling it the worst blizzard in history. Temperature dropped from sixty-five degrees to fifteen below zero in less than two hours."

"That's right. It did do that," Tennessee said. "I recollect I was down to the south pond and was warm enough that I was thinkin' about how nice and cool the water looked. Then the snow hit and I wasn't sure I would be able to find my way back to the bunkhouse. Then again, it wasn't that much better in the bunkhouse. The snow blew in through the cracks around the windows and between the boards so that by the next morning it was six inches deep on the floor."

Barry looked up from the paper. "Well, we weren't alone. According to this paper, no part of the western plains was spared," he said. Then he began to read the article aloud. "From Montana to Texas, ranchers lost upward of sixty to ninety percent of their cattle. Many cattlemen abandoned their ranches without any attempt to round up or rebuild their herds. It is estimated that twenty million cattle died.' "

Barry was quiet for a moment.

"What are you readin' now?" Tennessee asked.

Barry looked up from the paper with a sympathetic expression on his face. "It says lots of cowboys died, too, froze to death while they was trying to save the herd. They died for twenty dollars and found, workin' on ranches that was owned by folks who live back east somewhere. I doubt the ranch owners even knew the names of the cowboys who died for them."

"Yeah, well, at least Mr. Brookline knew Cal's name."

"That ain't the same thing. Mr. Brookline didn't own Trailback, if you recall. It was owned by some folks in England, and you can bet they didn't know Cal's name."

"That's true. But at least we come through it alive."

"I suppose we did, but when you get down to it, we aren't much better off than Cal and the others who died. We're nearly out of food, we don't have two pennies between us, and we can't get work anywhere."

Tennessee snorted. "Find somethin' else to read. Don't that paper have any good news in it?"

"I'll read the humor column," Barry suggested. He read for a moment, then chuckled.

"What is it?"

Again, Barry read aloud:

A missionary traveled to a far-off land where he encountered cannibals. Inquiring about Reverend Smith, his predecessor, the missionary was informed that the Reverend Mr. Smith was no longer among the living.

"Oh, that's too bad," the missionary says. "And did you not find him to be a tender-hearted man?"

"Yes," the cannibal chief answered, smiling, as he picked his sharpened teeth. "His heart was very tender. So was his liver."

Both men laughed. Then Barry put the paper down. He tapped his vest pocket, where the wire they had received from Jim was neatly folded. "You think that telegram we got was real? You think Frankie and Jim really have a job for us down in El Paso?"

"Well, they're pretty good boys," Tennessee replied. "And it ain't cheap to send a wire, so don't reckon they would get in touch with us if they didn't have something lined up."

"Yes, but the question is, what?"

"Does it matter?"

"Yes, it matters. What if they're planning on something that we want no part of?"

"What could there possibly be that we wouldn't want anything to do with?"

"Robbing a bank maybe? Or a stagecoach. Or a train."

Tennessee rubbed his chin. "If it was, would you be game for it?"

"Is that what it is?" Barry asked.

Tennessee shook his head. "I don't know," he answered. "I'm not saying it is. I was just wondering how you would feel about something like that."

Barry sighed. "Tell the truth, Tennessee, I'm not sure how I feel about it. I mean it's not something I ever gave much thought to before. But right now, with no money, no work, and nobody hiring, I can see how a fella might ride a crooked path. I know I wouldn't want to rob any person. I figure they're just like me, trying to stay alive. But a bank, a stagecoach, a train? Well, that wouldn't be exactly like you're taking money from any individual now, would it?"

"Maybe not, but stealing is stealing, no matter who you're doing it to. Besides which, once you start down that path it doesn't take a whole lot to wind up like one of those fellas we were just talking about."

"Getting hung, you mean?" Barry asked.

Tennessee nodded. "Yeah."

Barry snorted. "Well, don't get me wrong, I wasn't saying I was going to do it, or even that I would do it. I was mostly just talking, that's all."

"Maybe Jim and Frankie have something honest lined up for us," Tennessee suggested.

"Yeah, maybe," Barry said. He walked over

to one of the bunks, then stretched out in it. "I guess we'll be finding out in another couple days. Right now, I plan to take advantage of this bunk."

"Yeah," Tennessee said, crawling into one of the other bunks. "Me, too."

Chapter 5

When Chad Taylor awoke, he had no idea where he was. He knew he wasn't in the bunkhouse. When he felt the woman stir beside him, he remembered. He, his brother, Hank, and their pals Ken Keene, Gene Curry, and Eddie Quick were heading for El Paso in response to a telegram they had received from Jim Robison and Frankie Ford. The telegram offered employment, which the five cowboys had been without since the big winter freeze.

With their newfound fortune, gained through the horse race, the boys were almost ready to forget El Paso, or at least delay getting there while they celebrated with, as Eddie put it, "wine, women, and song." Then, with a laugh, he had added, "But for my token, you can leave out the song."

That was how Chad happened to wake up in a bed with a woman who was at least ten to fifteen years older than his own eighteen years. Because she was sleeping with her mouth open and a small string of spittle dribbling down her chin, Chad could see that she was missing a couple of teeth, while a third was broken. He wondered what there was about her that had attracted him last night. He closed his eyes, then opened them again, but her looks didn't improve. Surely the woman he had paid his two dollars to was younger and better-looking than this woman. Perhaps the one he had brought upstairs slipped away during the night and her place was taken by this creature.

His musing was interrupted by a loud and insistent pounding on the door. He heard his brother, Hank, shouting at him.

"Chad! Chad, you still in there? Wake up and get out here. Someone's done stole our poke!"

Springing out of bed, vaguely aware that the woman beside him was now stirring, Chad hurried into his clothes, then bolted out the door, carrying his boots and still buttoning his fly as he confronted his brother. "Are you sure?"

Gene, Ken, and Eddie were in the hall with Hank, looking as agitated as he was.

"Eddie, he's teasing, isn't he?" Chad asked as he pulled on first one boot, then the other.

Eddie shook his head. "No, kid, he ain't. I'm the one discovered it. I got restless this morning and went down to the livery to check on our horses, and got no farther than one foot in the door when the liveryman told me we had been robbed. So I turned right around and come back here for you fellas."

"Come on," Gene said. "Let's see what we can find out."

The five young men raced down the stairs, their boots clomping noisily on the steps. Then they ran out of the saloon and up the street toward the stable. Chad's head was spinning by the time they got there.

The liveryman was standing in the doorway, obviously expecting them and looking defensive. "I can't tell any of you no more than I already told this fella," he said, indicating Eddie.

"Well, you ain't told us," Hank said. "So tell it again."

"Like I said," the liveryman began, "I come in here this morning and seen stuff scattered all over the ground—carpetbags, bedrolls, saddlebags. When I seen that, I knew someone had broke in last night and went through ever'-one's belongin's."

"Mister, we had near three hundred dollars in them saddlebags," Gene growled. "I thought you was supposed to look out for things that was left here with you!"

"Three hundred dollars?" the liveryman gasped.

"That's right. And it was left in your safekeeping."

"This here ain't no bank," the liveryman retorted. "You ought to've had more sense than to leave money here. What do you think that sign is for?" He pointed to the wall, which displayed a large painted sign declaring, THIS ESTAB-LISHMENT RESPONSIBLE FOR HORSE AND TACK ONLY. NO OTHER VALUABLES TO BE LEFT HERE.

"Oh, damn," Ken said. "I didn't see that sign last night."

"Didn't none of us see it," Eddie said. "Wouldn't surprise me none if the son of a bitch didn't even put it up till this mornin'."

"I assure you, that sign has been up all along," the liveryman sputtered. "You can ask anyone in town, if you don't believe me."

"Let's get out of here," Hank said, disgustedly.

Dejected, the five cowboys saddled their horses, then rode out of town.

"Damn, we're no better off now than we were last week," Eddie said.

"We're worse off," Ken replied. "Last week we had what was left of our pay."

"That's true."

"It could be worse. At least we got that telegram offering us a job," Chad said.

"Yeah, I reckon so," Gene agreed. "But it galls me to have to show up in El Paso without a dime to our name."

"Maybe we won't have to," Eddie suggested.

"You got any way of gettin' around that?" Gene asked.

"I might have if you boys are game."

"I'm game," Hank said. "Whatever it is, I'm game."

"Me, too. Less'n it's robbin' a bank," Ken added with a chuckle. "I don't think I want to do that."

"I'm not talkin' about robbin' a bank," Eddie said. "I'm talkin' about robbin' a train."

"What?" the other four boys shouted as one.

"You gone plumb crazy, Eddie?" Gene asked. "A train's worse than a bank. At least a bank is sitting still."

"The train will be sitting still, too," Eddie said. "If we do it right."

"If we do it right?" Ken scoffed. "Tell me, Eddie, just how the hell do you rob a train right?"

"It can be done," Eddie insisted.

"I didn't ask if it could be done," Ken said.

"The James boys have robbed enough of 'em to show that it can be done. What I want to know is, how do you do it right?"

"Well, for one thing, we do it different from the James boys."

"Why? Seems to me like they were pretty successful with it."

"Yes, but they also did it so many times that they got famous for doin' it. I only want us to do it one time, just to get the money back that we got stole from us. Hell, there ain't nobody knows us around here, and we ain't never done nothin' like this before, so there ain't no way anyone's ever goin' to know who it was."

"I don't know," Ken said. "Seems to me like folks could get themselves killed doin' stuff like that."

"Not if we're real smart about it," Eddie insisted.

"If we were real smart about it we wouldn't be doin' it in the first place," Gene said.

"Chad, you ain't said nothin'," Eddie said. "What do you think about the idea?"

Chad had been listening in absolute shock. His brother and his friends were discussing the idea as if it were a real possibility, and he couldn't believe what he was hearing.

"What do I think about holding up a train?

The idea scares me to death. I hope you aren't serious."

"Oh, yes, I'm serious all right. And I know how to do it so that nobody gets hurt. Nobody on the train, and especially not one of us. I can guarantee it!"

"And just how can you guarantee it?" Gene asked. "What is this plan you have?"

"Gene, why are you even asking?" Chad said. "Don't listen to his plan! Can't you see that you'll just encourage him into thinking you're interested?"

When Gene didn't answer him, Chad appealed to his brother. "Hank? Tell him! Tell him this is a crazy idea!"

"Well, now, maybe it won't hurt just to hear what he has to say," Hank said.

Chad let out a long sigh of defeat and turned his head away to stare off into the distance. Eddie, encouraged by the interest of the others, started his explanation, and Chad could tell by Eddie's words and the tone of his voice that, in his mind, the proposal had already won acceptance. He was beyond trying to talk them into it, and was now explaining how it would be done.

"It'll be a snap," Eddie said. "All we have to do is pick us out a water tower that's not near a town or anything. Then we'll wait for a night train to come along. We don't even have to do nothin' to stop it, just wait for it to stop for water. It bein' a night train, all the passengers will be asleep, so none of them will be any problem. Now, when the train stops, we knock on the door of the express car and get them to open the door. All them express cars got safes, and you got to figure that every one of 'em's got from three to four hundred dollars in 'em. The folks inside the express car won't be expectin' nothin', 'cause train robbers don't generally brother with that little amount of money. And they ain't gonna put up no fight where they might get themselves hurt over somethin' that small. Hell, boys, it'll be easy as pie."

"You know, I've got to admit, Eddie, that sounds like something we might be able to pull off," Hank said. "They say the simplest plans is the best. What do you think, Chad?"

"I think it's a simple plan, all right. And anyone who'd do it would have to *be* simple. Hank, will you listen to yourself? Do you know what you are saying?"

"Yeah, I reckon I do know what I'm saying, little brother," Hank replied. "I'm saying I think we ought to do it."

"Chad, what's the harm?" Ken asked. "Who's going to get hurt? What's a few hundred dollars to a big railroad company?"

"Yeah," Gene added. "It's not like we were stealing from some person. I mean, this is a big company we're talking about, not some poor cowboy who's worked hard for his money. This ain't at all like what was done to us. Besides, all we want to do is get our money back."

"Why are we even worryin' about it? We got a telegram from Jim and Frank tellin' us there's work in El Paso. Let's just go there and do the job. Make our money the honest way."

Even as Chad pleaded his case, he knew he had already lost the argument.

"I'll tell you what, Chad. You don't have to go with us," Ken said by way of compromise. "The four of us will do it. You can wait somewhere else and we'll give you your cut, same as if you had done it with us."

"Yeah, that's all right by me," Eddie said.

Chad felt a cold chill run down his back, and he took a long, slow breath.

"No," he finally said, speaking so quietly that they could barely hear him. "If you boys are determined to do this, I'm going with you."

Hank laughed and slapped his brother on the back. "Well, now, wonderful!" he said. "That's the way it should be. The five of us, riding together."

The five cowboys sat on their horses in a ditch at the bottom of the track bed. The mournful whistle of the approaching train brought home to Chad Taylor exactly what he, his brother, and their three friends were about to do. Under dripping trees in the dark of night, with a cold rain spitting in his face, Chad tried one more time to talk the others out of it.

"Listen, fellas, I don't think we've considered the real consequences of this," he said. "We've had some fun thinking about it, sure, but it'll mark us as outlaws for the rest of our lives."

"Not if we don't ever do it no more," Eddie insisted.

"Chad, it's a little late to be bringin' that up now, don't you think?" Hank asked. "You should've told us before if you weren't in favor of doing this."

"Come on, Hank. What the hell do you think I've been telling you from the moment Eddie came up with this crazy scheme?"

"And we told you that you don't have to go through with it," Eddie said. "Now if you're all that squeamish, why don't you just ride over there in the dark and see if you can't find yourself a sugar tit or something to suck on while the rest of us men pull the job?"

"Take it easy on him, Eddie," Hank said. "He's got a right to feel the way he does." Hank looked at his brother. "But he's right, Chad. You don't have to go through with this."

Chad sighed. "I reckon I'll do it," he said, resolutely.

"You sure?" Ken asked. " 'Cause we can't have no more doubts now. It's too late for that. We're down to the nut cuttin'."

"I'm sure."

"Good man," Gene said, and he reached over to squeeze Chad on the shoulder. "Listen, I knew all along that he was going to go with us. He's never let us down before."

The loud shrill of a whistle indicated that the train was much closer now, and the steadily increasing noise made Chad's horse stamp its foot restlessly. Chad reached down to quiet his animal.

"Okay, boys, here she comes," Eddie said, the excitement of the moment creeping into his voice. He laughed. "Ain't we somethin'? Bet them James boys never pulled off a slicker holdup."

"We ain't pulled it off yet," Hank reminded him.

"We're about to. Pull your kerchiefs up over your nose, boys," Eddie said as he followed his own advice. "That way, nobody will be able to describe what you look like."

Chad stood up in the stirrups of his saddle and looked toward the approaching train. The headlamp was in view, its beam looking like a long yellow finger stabbing through the steadily falling rain. The puffing steam sounded like the gasps of some fire-breathing monster. And as if to add to the illusion, glowing sparks were being whipped away by the black smoke cloud that billowed up into the wet night sky.

"Get your guns out," Eddie ordered. "Soon as it stops for water, we'll go up and rap on the door of the express car. In five minutes we'll be ridin' away from here with three, maybe four hundred dollars in our poke."

Vented steam and squeaking metal sounded as the engineer began braking the train. Finally it rumbled and settled to a halt, with the tender poised just below the water tank. All the coach cars were dark, the passengers undoubtedly asleep just as Eddie had said they would be. That was good. Even though Chad had no experience in robbing a train, he was intuitive enough to realize that the greatest danger would come from the unexpected. And if the passengers were awake, the unexpected could happen.

"We made it here none too soon," Chad heard the fireman say as he crawled out onto the tender. "I'll bet you there ain't enough water left in this tank to work up a good spit." The tank's lid banged hollowly as the fireman dropped it open, then swung the spout over.

Chad shivered, but not from the cold.

"Here we go, boys," Eddie whispered. "Hank, you come with me. Rest of you fellas, stay down here in the ditch till they open the door. Soon as they open it, all of you fire a shot off in the air. That'll let 'em know there's too many of us for them to fight. They'll probably pee their pants, but you can bet they'll give up the money bag. I'll toss it down here: you fellas throw a few more shots in the air to keep them scared. Then we'll get the hell out of here." He grinned. "Simple."

Chad and the others drew their pistols as Eddie and Hank rode their mounts up to the top of the berm, making as little noise as possible. Down at the bottom of the gravel-covered embankment, Chad pointed his pistol straight up in the air and waited. His hands were sweating, and he could feel his heart pounding in his chest.

Suddenly he heard Eddie rap sharply on the door of the express car and call, "Hey! Hey, open up in there."

Chad glanced quickly toward the tender, but it was obvious that the fireman had heard nothing. The man's attention was on the water pouring into the tank, and the water was making such a roar that it covered all the other sounds.

The engineer stayed in his cab, surrounded by escaping steam and popping safety valves. Both fireman and engineer were oblivious to the drama being played out below them.

Chad watched as the express car door slid open, a narrow wedge of light growing to a large gap. A man appeared in the gap and looked outside. "What is it? What do you want?" he called into the darkness.

"Okay, let her go!" Eddie shouted, and Chad and the others fired into the air. The flashes of light from the gunshots painted the side of the express car orange, and the vivid scene seemed to freeze in Chad's brain for his most minute inspection.

"Throw down your money!" Eddie called.

"My God! It's a holdup! How did they know about the bank shipment?"

"Drop!" a loud voice called from farther back inside the car. The man in the doorway belly-flopped to the floor.

"What the hell is—" Eddie started to yell, but the loud roar and bright flash of a shotgun interrupted him. Chad saw Eddie tumble backward out of his saddle. His face was shot away.

"Oh, my God!" Chad screamed.

"Let's get the hell out of here!" Hank yelled. He managed to get his horse turned just before the second shotgun discharge. With that blast, a spray of blood, bone chips, and brain matter exploded from Hank's head as he went down.

"Hank!" Chad shouted. He started to dismount, but Gene reached over and grabbed him by the arm, physically keeping him in his saddle.

"You want to get killed, kid?" Gene shouted. "There's nothing you can do for your brother now!"

"Let's go!" Ken shouted, and he slapped Chad's horse on the rump.

The horse, already frightened by the shots, needed no further encouragement to bolt toward the rear of the train. Bending low over their horses' necks, the three men galloped away. Chad was the lightest and the best rider on the fastest horse. Not wanting to abandon them, he actually held his horse in check to keep from pulling away from them.

"There's three more and they're gettin' away!" someone shouted. "Shoot 'em! Shoot the sons of bitches!"

"I used up both barrels! I gotta reload!"

"Oh, Jesus, Jesus, Jesus," Chad heard himself crying out. He heard a couple of windows sliding open on the train, then a shot, not from a shotgun, but from a pistol. He didn't know if it was one of the guards in the express car or a passenger who happened to be armed and wanted in on the action.

When the three riders reached the end of the train, they kept going, following the track bed. The train was eastbound, and Chad, Ken, and Gene were heading west. Chad was reasonably sure that the guards wouldn't have horses aboard the train, but they couldn't take the chance. They kept pressing on for a long time to make certain that, if the trainmen did have horses, they wouldn't be able to catch them.

Finally, after they had ridden at least five miles with no sign of anyone following them, they stopped.

"If we don't want to kill these horses, we'd better walk them for a bit," Chad suggested, swinging down from the saddle.

"Yeah, good idea," Ken said. He looked behind them. "Doesn't look like anyone is following us."

Chad felt numb. He began leading Thunderbolt, talking soothingly to his horse but saying nothing to the others. He couldn't get rid of the picture of the gore spraying from the side of his brother's head.

"You all right, Chad?" Ken asked.

"No," Chad said, quietly. "No, I'm not all right."

"Were you hit?" Ken asked anxiously.

"I wish I had been. I wish I had been killed, along with Hank."

"No, you don't," Ken said. "You don't really mean that."

"How the hell do you know what I mean?" Chad snapped back at him.

"Come on, fellas," Gene said gently. "This is no time for us to be fightin' among ourselves. I'm real sorry about Hank, Chad. I'm sorry about Eddie, too."

"Yeah," Ken added. "Me, too. We shoulda listened to you."

Chad shook his head, then sighed. "It's not your fault," he said. "Eddie and Hank already had their minds made up to do this. I think they would've gone ahead and tried it whether we went along with them or not."

"The thing is, I believed Eddie's plan was a good one," Ken said. "You have to know that any normal train that's carrying no more than two or three hundred dollars, at the most, won't have guards."

"Yeah," Gene said. "It was just our luck that we chose to hit one that was carrying a bank shipment."

"What'll we do now?" Ken asked.

"We'll do whatever Chad wants to do," Gene said. "He was the only one of us who had enough sense to try and talk us out of the foolish mistake we just made. I'd say it's time we began listening to him."

"All right, Chad, what will it be?"

"Like I've been saying all along. We've got a telegram from Frank Ford and Jim Robison offering us work," Chad said. "I think that's where we ought to go now."

Without a word, Gene remounted, then turned away from the railroad track they had been following, heading off to the left.

"Where are you going?" Ken asked in surprise.

"We're goin' to El Paso, aren't we?" Gene asked. "It's this way."

Chapter 6

El Paso

The liveryman was working on the gate of the paddock when Barry Riggbee and Tennessee Tuttle rode up. Barry dismounted.

"We need to do a little business," Barry said.

The liveryman looked up. "Well, that's what we're here for. You fellas wantin' to board your horses?"

"Yes, and feed 'em," Barry replied. "Problem is, we don't have any money."

The liveryman pushed his hat back and ran his hand through a thick shock of hair that was brindled gray and black. "Maybe you boys don't understand how business is done. The thing is, I board and feed horses, but you have to pay money to have it done."

Barry nodded toward the gate. "I thought maybe we could fix that gate for you," he said, "and maybe take care of one or two other chores in exchange for feeding and boarding our horses."

"Uh-huh. And you'll be wantin' to stay in the stall with 'em, I suppose?"

Barry nodded. "Yeah, that, too," he answered sheepishly.

"Hell, mister, I wish I could help you, but I just work here," the stable man said. "If the boss comes by and finds you doin' my work, then I'm out of a job. You understand?" By way of dismissal, the liveryman went back to working on the gate.

"Yes," Barry said. He sighed. "Come on, Tennessee, we'll . . ."

"Wait a minute," the stable man said, looking up quickly. He nodded toward Tennessee. "Did you just call him Tennessee?"

"That's what he called me," Tennessee said. "My real name is Dan, but folks been callin' me Tennessee ever since I come out here."

"Would it be Tennessee Tuttle?" the liveryman asked.

"Yes," Tennessee replied, surprised that the liveryman seemed to know who he was.

"And you'd be Barry Riggsbee, I take it?"

"That's my name," Barry replied. "Say, what is this, mister? How is it that you know who we are?"

"Couple of friends of yours are in town," the liveryman said. "They said if you stopped by I was to put up your horses and feed 'em. So go ahead and leave them." He put his tools back down and rubbed his hands together. "What I mean is, they already paid for you two."

"Well, how about that?" Tennessee said, smiling broadly as he swung down from his horse. "That must've been Jim and Frank. Where are they now?"

The liveryman pointed toward one of the several saloons. "You might find 'em in any saloon in town, but it wasn't too long ago that I seen 'em go into the Border Oasis, and I ain't seen 'em come out."

"Thanks," Barry replied. He and Tennessee handed the reins of their mounts over to the liveryman, then started across the street toward the Border Oasis.

The liveryman started leading the horses into the barn. "Wisht I'da know'd who you was when you first made the offer," he said with a chuckle. "I'da took you up on it. I'da had you doin' my work, and I'da had the money, too."

*   *   *

The Border Oasis was filled with the odors of tobacco smoke, stale beer, and various alcoholic spirits. The drinking men, wearing wide-brimmed or high-crowned hats sat at tables, either playing cards or engaged in animated conversation. Half a dozen painted women, their hair adorned with feathers, ribbons, or sparkling glass jewelry, paraded about, their silk dresses rustling. Another dozen drinkers were at the bar, their spurred, high-heeled boots resting on a brass rail. Highly polished brass spittoons were placed at strategic places around the bar, though stains and bits of chewed tobacco were so prevalent in the sawdust on the floor that the spittoons seemed to serve a more decorative than functional purpose.

Jim Robison and Frank Ford were standing at the bar when Frank saw Barry and Tennessee in the mirror.

"Here come a couple of the boys," Frank said, nudging Jim. Smiling, he turned away from the bar and waved their two friends over to them.

"Well, I see you boys made it," Jim said. "Step up to the bar and have a drink with us."

"I'd love to, Jim. But if you had to pay a penny to wet your tongue, neither one of us could afford a smell," Tennessee answered.

"Oh, we can take care of that, can't we, Jim?" Frank said.

"We sure can," Jim said. "Go ahead and pay them."

"Pay us? Pay us what?" Barry asked.

Pulling out his wallet, Frank removed a stack of twenty dollar bills. He counted out five apiece to Tennessee and Barry.

"What is this?" Tennessee asked, looking at the notes.

Frank laughed. "That's money, my friend," he said. "One hundred dollars. Has it been so long since you saw any that you have forgotten what it is?"

"I mean, what is it for?"

"It's an advance against the work you're going to be doing," Jim explained. "That is, if you take the job."

"Hell yes, we'll take the job," Barry said. "What is it?" Then, with a chuckle, he added, "Wait a minute. I don't care what it is."

"No, you've got a right to ask," Jim said. "You ever heard of a fella named Clay Allison?"

"Sure, who hasn't?" Tennessee replied. "He's got himself quite a reputation with a gun."

"Wait a minute," Barry asked. "Jim, what does this have to do with Clay Allison? Is he hiring guns for a range war or something?"

Jim chuckled. "No, nothing like that. We're going to be wrangling horses for him. He's bought a herd, five hundred head, or so I'm told—from a fella down in Mexico. He's paying us two hundred dollars apiece to go get them. One hundred dollars now, and another hundred when we deliver the herd to his ranch just outside Alamosa, Colorado."

"Where do we find these horses?"

"Allison is sending a Mexican fella to guide us to where we're goin'."

"Who is this Mexican fella? You ever met him?"

"His name is Hector Ortega, and no, I haven't met him yet."

"Any of the other boys showed up to go yet?"

"Not yet," Jim answered. "But we've got three hundred dollars more to pay out in advances."

"What if nobody else shows? Couldn't we just split the advance money amongst ourselves?" Tennessee asked.

Jim shook his head. "Afraid not. When Allison brings Ortega to us, he will expect to see a body for every hundred dollars he's advanced. Anyway, I figure it'll take at least three more if we're going to do this, easy. If nobody else shows, I guess I'll just round up some of the locals, but I'd much rather have some of our own making the money. Truth to tell, I'm not all that pleased about havin' this Ortega fella go along with us. But I reckon if we're goin' to be poking around down in Mexico, it would be good to have someone with us who knows the country and speaks the lingo."

"Yeah, I guess you're right," Barry said. "Listen, if you don't need us anymore, I'm going to go see about a bath."

"Yeah, and a meal," Tennessee added.

"You boys go ahead," Jim said. "Have yourselves a good time tonight, but check back with us tomorrow."

"That when we're headin' out?" Barry asked. "Tomorrow?"

Jim nodded. "Looks that way. Allison said he would meet us, with Ortega, at the Border Oasis at noon on Saturday, the tenth of April. That's tomorrow."

Barry smiled broadly, then punched Tennessee on the shoulder. "See there? I told you I thought it was April," he said.

"That you did," Tennessee agreed. "Yep, it's just like I said. A man has no need of calendars when he's got ol' Barry Riggsbee around."

Jim and Frank laughed as their two friends left the saloon in search of a bath and food. They had just turned back to the bar when they heard a shout from one of the tables where a card game was in progress.

"What the hell? How the hell did you do that? I had two aces showing. How'd you know I didn't have 'em backed up?"

"You're not suggesting I'm a cheat, are you, Perkins?" one of the other players asked.

"No, no, of course not. It's just that I don't know how you can do that."

"Sounds like a pretty good game going on over there," Frank suggested.

"Pretty good for someone, I'd say," Jim agreed. When the two of them looked toward the gaming table, they saw a large, bald-headed, well-dressed man raking in a pile of chips.

"You want to know how I did this?" the bald man asked the player who had questioned him. "I did it by skill. You see, poker is eighty percent skill and twenty percent luck. It takes skill to run a bluff, and it takes skill to know when a bluff is being run. I always say that's what separates the men from the boys in this game. You, Perkins, are just a boy in a man's game."

Frank drank his whiskey and studied this skilled gambler for a moment. The bald man's eyes were brown and flashing brightly in the reflected light of the overhead lanterns.

The gambler chuckled happily, then continued.

"Boys, when you play with Mitch Jensen, you gotta expect to lose. But look at it like you was goin' to school, learnin' the game."

"Jensen, you're as full of shit as a Christmas goose," Perkins said.

"I may be a Christmas goose, Perkins," Jensen said as he shuffled the cards for another deal. "But you are a plucked hen."

Perkins looked chagrined as the others laughed. "Deal me out," he said.

Frank continued to study Jensen. Feeling Frank's steady gaze upon him, Jensen put his finger to his collar and pulled it away from his thick neck. Frank's eyes bore into him so that he had to look around.

"Can I help you, mister?"

Frank nodded toward the table. "Private game?"

Jensen smiled. "Private game? Hell, if you got the money to lose, I'll be glad to take it."

Frank turned toward Jim. "What do you think about playing with Allison's money?" he asked.

"Go ahead," Jim said. "But if you're going to do that, I'd rather you not lose."

Frank smiled. "I'll do my damnedest not to. You sort of keep an eye on things."

"Sounds like a good plan to me," Jim said as he lifted his drink.

Frank walked over to the table. When he arrived, Jensen looked over at Perkins. "You've taken yourself out of the game, Perkins. Get up and give the man your seat"—Jensen looked at Frank—"unless you feel the chair is unlucky."

"There are no unlucky chairs," Frank replied as he started toward the table. "Just unfortunate players."

Jensen laughed again. "Unfortunate players," he repeated. "Yes, to be sure. Well, let's see whether you will be fortunate or"—he paused for a moment before he let the last word slide out—"unfortunate."

Frank pulled the chair out, then sat down.

"You do have money?" Jensen asked.

When Frank put two hundred dollars on the table, some of the other players whistled softly.

"Well, now," Jensen said as he watched Frank make neat stacks of the bills in front of him. "Yes, I think you will make a fine addition to the game. And your money will be a fine addition to my wallet," he added with a laugh.

As he had discussed with Jim, the two hundred dollars Frank was playing with came from the money they were carrying to be advanced to anyone who agreed to go to Mexico with them. It was a risky operation but Frank had a feeling about Jensen. Jensen was a little too overconfident, and it had been Frank's experience that overconfident gamblers could be taken.

Jensen picked up the cards, but Frank waved his finger back and forth. "There's a new player at the table," he said. "I have the right to call for a new deck."

"A new deck? All right," Jensen said, picking up a fresh box. Using his thumbnail, he broke the seal, then took the cards out. Removing the joker, he spread the deck out on the table, then turned the cards over expertly in one motion. He was quite dextrous and made a little show of it for Frank. "Are you satisfied with the cards?" he asked.

"Deal them," Frank said.

Jensen shuffled the cards and the stiff new pasteboards clicked sharply. His hands moved swiftly, folding the cards in and out, until the law of random numbers became the law of the table. He shoved the cards toward Frank, who cut them, then pushed them back.

"Is five-card draw all right with you?" Jensen asked.

"Five-card draw is fine."

Frank lost fifteen dollars on the first hand, folding cautiously with a hand that would have been good enough to win had he stayed in the game.

Jensen laughed as he dragged in the pot.

"This isn't a game for the weak of heart, stranger," he said. "You should've bet the hand."

Frank lost the second hand the same way, and again Jensen laughed.

By the third hand, Frank was down thirty-five dollars, but there was over sixty dollars in the pot, and he had drawn two cards to complete a heart flush. He bet five dollars.

"Careful now, mister," Jensen warned. "You don't want to get carried away here. I'll see your five, and raise you five."

Frank made a big show of studying his hand carefully. Finally, as if only after careful consideration, he called, but didn't raise Jensen's bet.

"All right, cowboy, let's see what we have," Jensen said. Jensen was holding three kings, and he laughed when he saw Frank's hand.

"A flush? You were holding a flush and all you did was call?"

"You might've had a flush with a bigger card. I like to be certain about things. As you can see, it paid off," Frank said as he raked in the pot. "I am now forty dollars ahead."

"It paid off, did it?" Jensen asked. "Because you're a lousy forty dollars ahead in the game?"

Jensen's vanity was piqued at the thought of

a rank amateur taking the pot. Frank had counted on that. He planned to make this an interesting game.

"I'm going to ante the limit this time," Frank said hesitantly. He put his hand on the money and held it for a moment, as if thinking about it. Then, with a sigh, he pushed the money forward. "Ten dollars."

"Oh, ten dollars?" Jensen teased. "We're getting into some heavy money now. What do you say we up the ante a little?"

"Up the ante?" Frank asked.

"You say your system is paying off. Let's up the ante and see," Jensen challenged.

"All right, if you want to," Frank replied, still talking as if he were being manipulated by Jensen.

"That's more like it," Jensen said. He shoved the cards across the table to Frank. "Here, it's your deal."

When Frank picked up the cards, he felt them as he began shuffling, checking for pinpricks and uneven corners. They were playing with an honest deck. He smiled. Evidently Jensen was so sure of himself that he felt no need to cheat in this game. And of course, Frank had played his hands in a way that would tend to support Jensen's belief.

Frank dealt the cards. The betting was quite

brisk and within a few moments the pot was over two hundred dollars.

"Now, cowboy, I'm afraid it's going to cost you to see what I have," Jensen said. He slid a stack of chips to the center of the table. "One hundred dollars."

Jensen's bet was high enough to run everyone else out of the game, and he chuckled as he gazed across the table at Frank.

"What about it, mister? It's just you and me now. You want to pay to see what I've got?"

Frank studied his cards for a long moment.

"Come on, mister, you can't take all night," Jensen said. "What're you going to do?"

"I'll see your one hundred, and raise it one hundred," Frank said.

Jensen gasped, and he looked at Frank in openmouthed surprise.

"What kind of hand do you have, mister?" he asked.

"A pretty good one, I think," Frank answered. He put the cards down in front of him, four to one side, and one off by itself.

"Son of a bitch, he's got four of a kind," someone said. "Look at the way he put his cards down."

"I'll tell you this, whatever the man had, there's over three hundred dollars in that pot," another said.

By now the stakes of the game were high enough to attract the attention of everyone else in the saloon, and there were several men standing around the table, watching the players with intense interest. Only Jim hadn't come over to join them. He remained back at the bar, ostensibly uninterested in the game. In reality, he was keeping a close eye on everyone and everything, covering Frank's back. It was a procedure they had developed long ago.

"He's bluffin', Jensen," Perkins said. "Hell, I can tell by lookin' at him that he's bluffin'. Call his hand."

Jensen snorted. "I'm supposed to listen to you? You've already proved how good a poker player you are," he said sarcastically.

"Call him," Perkins urged again.

"It's my money you're talkin' about," Jensen said. "You give me one hundred dollars, and I'll call him."

"I already gave you a hundred dollars," Perkins said. "You won that much from me today."

"Yeah, well, it's mine now, and I don't plan to throw it away." He rubbed his chin as he studied Frank. "And don't forget, this is the fella who wouldn't even raise a flush."

Frank's face remained impassive.

"What are you going to do, Jensen?" one of the bystanders asked. "Like you told this gentleman a few moments ago, you can't take all night."

"All right, all right, the pot's yours," Jensen said, turning his cards up on the table. He had a full house, aces over jacks. "What have you got?"

Frank's cards stayed facedown on the table just the way he left them, four in one pile, one in another. He reached out to rake in his pot.

"I asked you a question, mister. What have you got?" Jensen asked again. He reached for Frank's cards, but Frank caught him around the wrist with a vise grip.

"Huh-uh. You didn't pay to see them," Frank said easily.

With his other hand, Jensen slid some money across the table. Frank saw two twenties and a ten.

"Is that enough to let me see?"

"All right, if you want to," Frank said. He let go of Jensen's wrists, and Jensen turned up the cards. Instead of four of a kind, there were two small pairs.

"What the hell is this?" Jensen gasped, glancing up from the cards with an expression of exasperation on his face. "You beat me with two pairs?"

"Won't two pairs beat a full house?"

"No, you idiot!"

"Oh. Well, then, I guess I just don't understand the game that well," Frank said innocently.

The others around the table laughed uproariously, not sure whether Frank was telling the truth or if he was perpetrating a gigantic hoax on Jensen.

Frank started to pick up the money. "Gentlemen, it's been fun, but now I must go—"

"Just a minute! Hold it! Where do you think you are going? You aren't leaving the table with those winnings."

"Then I guess I really don't understand the game," Frank said. "I thought we were playing for keeps."

"We are playing for keeps," Jensen sputtered. "But if you play with me, you don't walk away without giving me a chance to get even."

"Is that a fact? Then remind me never to play with you again." Frank began stuffing the money into his pockets.

"Better do somethin', Jensen. That feller's gettin' away with your money," Perkins teased.

"It's your money, too," Jensen said.

"Not anymore it ain't. Now it's all his. And truth to tell, if I can't get it back I'd rather the stranger have it than you."

Perkins's declaration was followed by even more laughter.

With his pockets now bulging with money, Frank started toward the bar. In the meantime, in a move unnoticed by nearly everyone, Jensen made a slight signal to a man who was standing near the rail at the overhead landing.

Jensen might have thought that he gave the signal unnoticed, but Jim saw it. When Jim looked up, he saw someone on the upstairs landing pointing his pistol at Frank.

"Frank, look out!" Jim shouted.

Jim's warning was barely in time. Frank dived to the floor just as the upstairs gunman fired. The bullet punched a hole in the floor beside Frank's sprawled form.

Realizing that his target had been warned by the man standing at the bar, the gunman swung his pistol toward Jim, squeezing the trigger as he did so. His bullet crashed into the mirror behind the bar, leaving jagged shards to reflect grotesquely twisted images of the events taking place before it.

Frank was not the only person who had dived to the floor. By the time the gunman had fired a second shot nearly everyone else in the saloon was on the floor, behind chairs, or under tables. The only one who was still standing upright was Jim Robison and by now he had his own pistol out. His first shot rang out just over the top of the gunman's third shot. The gunman's third shot smashed into the bar, splintering the mahogany. Jim's shot caught the gunman in the middle of the chest. Startled, the would-be assassin dropped his pistol, then put both hands over his wound, trying to stem the flow of blood spilling through his fingers. He reeled for a moment, fighting hard to stay on his feet. Losing that battle, he pitched forward, smashing through the rail. Falling to the floor below, his body did a half flip on the way down before crashing belly-up through a table.

"You all right?" Jim called to his cousin.

"Yeah, I'm fine," Frank answered.

The shooting drew a crowd, not only from those who were already in the Border Oasis, but from the rest of the town as well. For the next few minutes a steady stream of curious poured in through the front door. One of the first to arrive was the sheriff, and he saw Jim standing at the bar with his pistol in his hand.

"You want to put that way, mister?" the sheriff asked.

When Jim looked toward the sheriff, he saw that the lawman was holding a pistol on him.

"Anything you say, Sheriff," Jim said, slipping his pistol back in its holster.

"Now are you the one who did this?" the sheriff asked, taking in the body with a nod.

"I reckon I am."

"He didn't have no choice, Sheriff," the bartender said. "It was self-defense."

"That's right, Sheriff," several others said, quickly. "Creech fired first."

The sheriff thought for a moment, then put his gun away. "What's your name?" he asked.

"Robison. Jim Robison."

The sheriff looked at the shattered mirror, the splintered bar, the smashed table, and the broken railing hanging in pieces from the overhead landing.

"Must've been one hell of a fight. Looks like more bullets were fired in here than were used at the Alamo."

"Only four shots were fired," one of the saloon patrons said.

"Only four? Someone want to tell me what happened?"

About five people started speaking at once, each eager to give his own account of the battle.

"Hold it, hold it!" the sheriff said, interrupting the babble. He looked at the bartender. "Did you see it, Ned?"

"Yeah, I seen it."

"All right, suppose you tell me what happened?"

"Creech took one shot at this man," Ned said, pointing to Frank. "When Robison called him on it, Creech swung his gun around and took another couple of shots at him. Robison shot back."

The sheriff looked down at Creech's body, then up at the smashed railing, then over toward the bar.

"You got him with your first shot?" the sheriff asked.

"I was lucky," Jim said easily.

"Wasn't luck at all," the bartender said. "I seen it. You was cool as a cucumber."

"What started the fight in the first place?" the sheriff asked. "I mean, all of you say Creech fired first. What I want to know is, why?"

"Now that I don't know," the bartender replied. "There wasn't no words spoke or nothin'. Leastwise, not in here. Could be they had words somewhere else before."

"You know this man?" the sheriff asked Jim.

"Never saw him before in my life."

The sheriff looked over at Frank. "What's your name?"

"Frank Ford."

"What about you, Ford? Why did he shoot at you? Did you know him?"

Frank shook his head no. "Like my cousin said, we don't know him."

"The two of you are cousins?"

"Yes."

"Well, then that tells me why you was willin' to take a hand in this fella's fight," the sheriff said. "But it still don't tell me why there had to be a fight in the first place."

"Ask the gambler there," Jim said. "Jensen gave Creech the signal to dry-gulch Frank. I saw it and yelled a warning. That's when Creech started firing."

"What? Why, that's preposterous!" Jensen shouted angrily.

"Anyone else see this signal?" the sheriff asked. "What about you, Ned? Did you see any kind of a signal?"

"I didn't see no signal," Ned said. "I don't know why Creech started shootin'. All I know is, he was the one who fired the first shot."

"You know how Creech was, Sheriff. He always was a bit strange Maybe he just went loco or somethin'. If this here fella hadn't killed him, no tellin' how many of us Creech would've shot," one of the other patrons suggested.

"Yes, including me, a totally innocent by-stander," Jensen insisted.

"Creech worked for you, didn't he, Jensen?" the sheriff asked.

"What? No, he didn't work for me. Whatever gave you that idea?"

"Funny. I seem to recall you usin' him as a bodyguard."

"Well, I would use him from time to time, but only if I was in a big game where there was a lot of money involved," Jensen insisted. "He didn't work for me regular. And certainly not for this game. Why, this game was for a pittance. I hardly thought it necessary to hire a bodyguard."

"The last pot was for nearly four hundred dollars," Perkins said. "That's hardly a pittance."

"That may be a large pot to you, Perkins, but I have played for thousands of dollars," Jensen said haughtily.

The sheriff stroked his chin for a moment, then looked over at Jim. "Mr. Robison, everyone seems to back up your claim that it was self-defense, so I don't aim to arrest you. But as far as Jensen sendin' a signal, well, don't nobody else seem to have seen that, so I reckon we'll just have to let that drop."

By now the undertaker had arrived and he was bending over to examine to corpse.

"Welch, get the body out of here," the sheriff said to the undertaker. "It ain't good for business."

"The city will pay for it?" Welch asked.

The sheriff nodded in the affirmative, then he looked toward Jim and Frank. "Didn't have no trouble till you two boys showed up. You planning on staying in town long?"

"Just overnight," Jim answered. "We're meeting someone here tomorrow."

"Someone local? Who is it you are meeting?"

"Clay Allison."

There were several gasps and exclamations of surprise at the mention of the famous gunman's name.

"Look here," the sheriff asked, his eyes narrowing. "You two aren't planning on shootin' it out in my town, are you?"

Jim laughed. "Sheriff, I've been called a lot of things in my life, but dumb isn't one of them. I don't plan to go up against Clay Allison in this town, or any other. We're just going to discuss some business, that's all."

"Uh-huh," the sheriff responded. It was obvious that he was still suspicious of Jim. "Well, you and Clay Allison go on about your business. But just so's you know, I plan to put on a few extra deputies to keep a watch on you."

Chapter 7

Clay Allison once wrote an indignant letter to the editor of a Missouri newspaper. The paper had published a story that accused him of fifteen killings.

I have at all times tried to use my influence toward protecting the property holders and substantial men of the country from thieves, outlaws, and murderers, among whom I do not care to be classed.

It was noted by all who read the letter, that Allison had not actually denied the killings.

His reputation for savagery was validated when he rounded up a handful of friends to lynch a rancher who had been accused of killing his own infant daughter. The rancher had been arrested and was in jail, awaiting the outcome of the investigation, but Allison needed no investigation to reach his conclusion.

Under Allison's leadership, the rancher was hauled out of his jail cell, taken to a nearby slaughterhouse, and lynched. Then Allison beheaded the corpse, stuck the rancher's head on a sharpened stick, and took it to the next town, where it was put on display behind the bar of his favorite saloon.

He once killed a man who was standing at a bar because the man fanned his face with his hat. Allison's defense was: "He was fanning his face with his left hand, and it wasn't a warm night. I believed the man was attempting to distract me so he could draw his pistol and kill me." The court bought his argument and ruled the killing as a justifiable homicide.

Even as Jim, Frank, Barry, and Tennessee were waiting in El Paso for Clay Allison, the notorious gunman was some twenty miles away at a livery stable in Le Mesa, New Mexico, seeing about his horse.

"Feed him well tonight, Mañuel," Clay ordered. "I have to ride over to El Paso tomorrow to conduct some business."

"Sí, senor," the Mexican liveryman replied.

"I've been looking for Hector Ortega. Do you know where he is?"

"I think maybe you will find him over at the

cantina. I did not see him there, but I think that's where he will be."

"Thanks."

As Clay started toward the Mexican side of town, he walked not on the sidewalk as most pedestrians would, but in the middle of the street. Choosing such a path meant he had to be particularly watchful for wagon and horse traffic, as well as for horse droppings, but this particular habit made a surprise ambush from behind a building less likely.

As soon as he crossed the railroad tracks into the barrio, the texture of the town changed as drastically as if he had left one city and gone to another. Here, among the small adobe buildings that housed the Mexicans and their families, the nights were darker, for only the cantina was well lighted. The other structures were either awash in total darkness or barely illuminated by burning embers of mesquite or fat-soaked rags. That was because few could afford candles and fewer still, kerosene lanterns.

There were no hotels in the barrio and no restaurants. The largest building was the cantina, and from inside that brightly lit edifice, Clay Allison could hear someone singing, accompanied by a guitar. Clay spoke no Spanish, so he had no idea what the song was about, but it did have a lilting melody that he liked. He once made the observation that those who sang Mexican music had to have a very good voice because of the trills and warbles of the wide-ranging melodies.

Although the church was the center of all social life in the barrio, the cantina ran a close second. Here, a man could eat, drink, and if so inclined, meet whores. Although the *putas* would meet their customers in the cantina, they generally carried on the trade from their own houses. In many cases the whores had children who were comfortable with their mother's occupation simply because they knew of no other existence.

Most of the *putas'* customers were Mexican workers who couldn't afford—or have been welcomed by—the Anglo whores. However, many of the customers were American—some attracted to the women because of their dusky beauty, others because a Mexican whore cost less than half as much as an Anglo.

Generally, if an Anglo man visited a cantina, it was for that purpose and no other. Therefore, when Clay set foot inside the door he was immediately met by one of the women. Hiking her skirt up above a shapely leg, she put her foot on a chair, her elbow on her knee, then leaned forward to put her chin on her hand. Such a pose not only showed her leg, but accented her curves and displayed a generous amount of cleavage.

"I am Carmine," the woman said.

Clay didn't answer. Instead, he stood just inside the door, surveying the room.

"Senor, you do no need to look for another," Carmine said. "I will be your woman"—she paused for a moment, then flashed a big smile—"for the right price."

"Thank you, but I'm not looking for a woman," Clay said. "I am looking for a man named Hector Ortega."

When he said Hector's name, two men stepped away from the bar. Like nearly every other Mexican in the place, they were wearing high-crowned, large-brimmed sombreros. They were also wearing pistols, and one of them had a rather large knife protruding from a sheath that was strapped diagonally across his chest.

"Gringo, why do you look for Senor Ortega?" the one with the knife asked. The inquiry was more of a challenge than a question.

"I reckon why I want to see him is my business," Clay replied. His reply was equally challenging.

"I think maybe we will kill you. And then it

will be nobody's business," his other challenger said.

At those words the guitar music suddenly ended on a jarring chord. All conversation in the cantina stopped as well, and everyone stared at Clay and the two who had confronted him.

Clay fixed his adversaries with a cold, mirthless smile. "If you hombres are planning on doin' anything, let's get to it," he said in a calm voice. He moved his hand slightly, so that it hovered just over the handle of his pistol.

At that moment the back door opened and Hector Ortega, who had been outside visiting the *tocador*, returned to the cantina. He was still tucking his shirttail into his trousers when he saw Clay Allison and the two men from the bar bracing each other. He saw, also, that the cantina had grown deathly quiet.

"Senor Allison, welcome, amigo!" he said expansively. Smiling and extending his hand, he started toward the American. As he walked by the two men who had confronted Clay, he spoke to them in Spanish, from the side of his mouth.

"Los absurdos! Ustedes desean ser matado? Ésta es Clay Allison."

The two "foolish ones" blanched visibly.

"Senor Allison, we did not know you were Hector's amigo," the one with the knife said. He extended his hand but, pointedly, Clay turned away from him, motioning to Ortega to step out front so they could hold a private conversation.

"Have you heard from the people down in Durango?" Clay asked once they were outside.

"Sí. The horses are ready."

"Good. Tomorrow, we'll ride over to El Paso. By then Robinson and Ford will have put together an outfit to go after the horses with you. I'm putting you in charge, Ortega."

"*Gracias*, senor."

"Now, they're probably not going to like that," Clay said. "I mean, you being Mexican and all. But I figure it's your country and your language, so by rights, you should be the trail boss. All I'm asking is that you do a good job for me."

"Do not worry, senor We will bring all the horses back in good shape," Ortega promised.

"I figure you will. Otherwise I wouldn't hire you." Clay looked back toward the front of the cantina. "I'm going back over to my side of town now to have supper. I'd appreciate it if you would watch my back till I'm out of here. I'm not sure I trust those two hombres inside."

"I will watch out for you," Ortega said.

Returning to the American side of town, Clay went into the Longhorn Restaurant. As he stepped inside the door he was met by the café owner. "Mr. Allison," the proprietor said nervously. "Do you know that gentleman over there?"

Clay looked in the direction the proprietor indicated. There, sitting at a table in the far corner of the room, was a man who stood out from the rest of the patrons. Whereas most of the other diners were wearing denim trousers and cotton shirts, this man was wearing a three-piece suit, complete with silk cravat and diamond stickpin. Perhaps a few years younger than Clay, he also sported a neatly trimmed Vandyke beard.

"No, I can't say as I do know him."

"He has been waiting to see you. He asked that I seat you at his table. He also said I was to serve you anything you wished, because he would pay for it."

Clay smiled, then put his hat on the hatrack. "Is that so? Well, maybe he's a businessman wanting to buy some horses. All right, I'll have steak, eggs, potatoes, biscuits, butter, and some peach jelly."

"Very good, sir."

When Clay reached the back table, the stranger stood and amicably extended his hand. The moment he did so, Clay's perception of him as a potential business prospect changed. The man was wearing a pistol with the holster low and tied down. The skirt of his jacket was kicked back to allow a quick draw. This wasn't normal for a businessman.

"Mr. Allison, my name is Chunk Colbert," the man said. "Have you ever heard of me?"

"Chuck Colbert? No, I can't say as I have."

"Not Chuck, Chunk," the man corrected.

Clay smiled. "Unusual name," he said.

"Yes, sir, I suppose it is," Colbert agreed. "I'm a little disappointed you haven't heard of me. You see, it's a name folks are beginning to take notice of."

"And why is that, Mr. Colbert?"

Colbert flashed a toothy smile. "Because I've killed seven men in fair gunfights."

Clay's eyes narrowed. "You've killed seven men, you say."

"Yes, sir."

"And you are proud of that?"

"I am, sir. Every one of those fights have been open and aboveboard."

"Why did you kill them?"

"Why? Well, I don't know that I can give you a reason for every one of them," Colbert said. "But then I'm sure you understand. From what I hear, you've killed a lot more men than I have."

"I've never killed anyone, Mr. Colbert, who didn't need killing," Clay said.

"Would you say that someone who is trying to kill you would need killing?"

"Well, yes, but there has to be more to it than that. I mean, someone wouldn't be trying to kill you unless they had a reason."

"It could be that they are just trying to get their name a little better known."

"That's foolish."

"That's easy for you to say, Allison. There's not a man in the country, from New York to San Francisco, who doesn't know your name, who doesn't tell exciting stories of your exploits."

"Maybe so. But I haven't sought such fame."

"Then that is where we differ, Mr. Allison, because, you see, it *is* something I seek," Colbert said. "That's why I'm going to kill you, tonight."

"What?" Clay asked in surprise.

"Oh, not right this minute," Colbert said quickly. He smiled, then held his hand out, offering a seat to Clay. "At least, not until after we have had our supper. I told the proprietor that your meal would be on me. I hope you ordered."

"I did order," Clay said. "After you," he added, indicating that Colbert should take his seat first.

Colbert laughed. "I can see how you have survived as long as you have, Mr. Allison. You are a cautious man." Colbert sat down, then Clay sat across from him. Clay's food was brought to the table.

"Since you are buying the supper, I'd like for you to pay the man now, if you don't mind," Clay said. "I wouldn't want anyone to see me going through your pockets afterward and think I had shot you for your money."

Colbert blanched for just a second. Then he laughed. "Very good, Mr. Allison, very good," he said. "You are trying to make me nervous. I think I'll just borrow that little trick from you, since you won't be needing it anymore after to-night" He removed his billfold from his inside jacket pocket, then took out the money to pay for the meal and handed it to the waiter. "There, your supper is all paid for. Plus a generous tip for the waiter."

"Thank you," Clay replied.

Over the next several minutes the two men enjoyed a leisurely meal. They exchanged stories and laughed so frequently that anyone watching might think they were two longtime friends catching up on old times.

The other diners knew better, however, because some of them had overheard the initial conversation between the two men. They had passed it on to others until soon, everyone in the restaurant knew. Word spread beyond the cafe as well, so that before Clay Allison and Chunk Colbert were finished with their supper, every table was filled and there were many more present who were standing along the walls, watching. As a result of the unfolding drama, all other conversation in the cafe had stopped as everyone waited, silently, to see what was going to happen.

Oddly, Clay Allison and Chunk Colbert were not aware that the other conversations had stopped, or that they were the objects of such close scrutiny. They were so intent on the business at hand that they were oblivious to the large and deathly silent crowd.

As the last of the apple pie was eaten, Colbert signaled the waiter to pour them each another cup of coffee. The waiter did so, then withdrew quickly. Neither Clay nor Colbert noticed that the waiter's hands were shaking.

"Mr. Allison, it has been a most enjoyable experience," Colbert said. "I drink to our newfound but, of necessity, short-lived friendship, sir."

As Colbert reached for his coffee cup, Clay saw that he was reaching for the cup with his left hand. Since Colbert had been using his right hand throughout the meal, that put Clay on in-

stant alert. He gripped the handle of his pistol
and waited.

As the cup was halfway up to his mouth, Colbert suddenly drew his pistol with his right
hand. Seeing this, Clay pulled his own gun at
the same time. Colbert tried to whip his gun up
into firing position, but he failed to compensate
for the tabletop. The pistol sight caught the bottom of the table, preventing him from getting
the gun any higher. In desperation, he fired anyway, but the bullet missed. By now, Clay had
his own pistol up and clear of the table, and
had an unobstructed shot. His gun flashed and
roared. A small black hole pushed through just
above Colbert's right eye. Colbert's chair pitched
over backward with the would-be assassin dead
before he could hit the floor.

Even before the smoke cleared, Clay was on
his feet, looking down at the sprawled body of
Chunk Colbert, making certain that the shot was
fatal. It wasn't until he was totally satisfied that
Colbert no longer represented any danger to
him, that he glanced up. He gasped in surprise
at the number of people who were there, looking at him in wide-eyed, openmouthed awe.

Clay punched the empty casing out of the cylinder of his pistol, then slid another bullet into
the chamber. Holstering his pistol, he signaled
the proprietor over.

"Why are there so many people here?" he asked quietly.

"Someone overheard Mr. Colbert challenge you," the proprietor replied. "Word spread that there was going to be a shoot-out. These people came to watch."

"The hell you say," Clay said. He started to put the empty cartridge in his pocket.

"I will give you ten dollars for that cartridge," the proprietor said.

Clay looked surprised. "Ten dollars?"

"Yes, sir."

Clay smiled. "Mister, you just bought yourself one worthless piece of brass," he said, handing the shell casing to him.

The proprietor took a ten-dollar bill from his wallet. "Mr. Allison, there is one thing I don't understand," he said. "If you knew Colbert was going to try and kill you, why did you agree to have supper with him? I mean, the two of you sat at the table and ate as if you were old amigos. There were some who left, believing the whole thing might be a hoax."

"I ate supper with him because I didn't want to send him to hell on an empty stomach," Clay replied.

The proprietor laughed nervously. "Yes, to be sure, one wouldn't want to go to hell on an empty stomach," he said.

Clay started for his hat. "I believe the bill is all settled?"

"Yes, sir, thank you."

"Then I must be going. I've a long ride ahead of me in the morning." He got to the door, then looked around at the crowded restaurant. Most were still staring at him. Clay held up his hand. "Oh, you folks really should try the apple pie," he said. "It is absolutely excellent."

Not until he left the cafe did the crowd regain its voice. Everyone began talking at the same time, sharing what they had seen. As Clay walked up the sidewalk toward the hotel, he could hear the cacophonous babble behind him.

It wasn't until that moment that the nervousness hit him, and his knees grew so weak that he reached out to the edge of the building to steady himself. He stood there for a long moment, taking deep breaths until he had regained his composure.

Chapter 8

El Paso was bustling when the three young cowboys rode into town on the morning of April tenth. Two trains were standing in the depot. One was a passenger train taking on travelers for its run back east. Even though the engineer was at rest, the fireman wasn't. He was working hard, stoking the fire to keep the steam pressure up.

In contrast to the fireman's toil, the engineer was leaning out the window of the highly polished, green-and-brass locomotive. He was smoking a curved-stem pipe as he watched the activity on the depot platform, serene in the power and prestige of his position.

A score of passengers was boarding or getting off the train as the conductor stood beside the string of varnished cars, keeping a close check on the time. Over on the sidetrack sat a second train. That one was a freight, its relief valve puffing as the steam pressure was maintained. The passenger train had priority over the "high iron," as the main track was called, and only after it departed would the freight move back onto the main line in order to continue its travel west.

Two stagecoaches and half a dozen carriages were also sitting at the depot, while out in the street behind the depot a horse-drawn streetcar rumbled by.

As Chad, Gene, and Ken rode through the town, they looked into the faces of everyone they encountered, studying them for any reaction to their presence.

"It don't look like anyone's takin' any particular notice of us," Ken said. "Maybe don't nobody know we're train robbers."

"More'n likely, they haven't even heard about it in the first place, seein' as how we ain't really train robbers. Don't forget, the train robbery never come off," Gene said. "I don't see no need to be worried."

"And anyway, nobody saw us. We were down in the ditch, in the dark," Ken insisted.

"Nobody saw us, that's true. But they may

find out who Hank and Eddie are," Chad said. "And if they do, it won't take much to connect them with us, 'specially since Hank was my brother."

"So what are you saying, Chad? That we should just stop livin'? That we should run away and hide somewhere?" Gene asked.

"No, I'm not sayin' that a'tall. But I don't think we should ever talk about it. Don't tell the other boys about it, and let's not even talk about it among ourselves anymore, in case someone might overhear us," Chad said.

"Oh, hell, I'll go along with that," Ken said. "What we done was so damn stupid, it ain't somethin' I'd ever want to tell anyone about, anyway."

"Hey, there's Barry Riggsbee!" Gene said, pointing to a man walking down the sidewalk. "Barry!" he called.

Hearing his name shouted, Barry looked toward the street, then smiled when he saw the three cowboys weaving their way through the heavy street traffic, working their way over to him.

"I see you got the telegram," Barry said, greeting them as they dismounted to shake his hand. "Me an' Tennessee both got one, too, telling us to come here."

"That's what ours says as well. Have you seen Jim and Frankie yet? Are they in town?"

"They're not only in town—they've got money for anyone who signs up for the job. Me'n Tennessee have already got ours."

"Where are they?"

"I'd try the Border Oasis if I was you. That's a saloon just down the street. They're supposed to meet Clay Allison there sometime today, so I reckon they'll be hanging around there till he shows."

"Who?" Ken asked.

"Clay Allison. Haven't you ever heard of him?"

"Of course I've heard of him. What's he got to do with anything?"

"Well, if you take the job the telegram was talking about then you're going to be working for him. We all are. Seems he's bought some horses he wants us to bring up from Mexico."

"What's he paying?" Gene asked.

"That's the best part," Barry answered. "He's paying two hundred dollars apiece, and like I told you, you'll get the first hundred soon as you agree to hire on."

"Have you and Tennessee hired on?" Chad asked.

"Yep. So far there's Tennessee and me, Jim

Robison, and Frank Ford. And now you three, if you're goin' to do it."

"Hell yes, we're going to do it," Chad said.

"Good, good. Glad we'll be working together again. By the way, how's your brother gettin' along? And where's Eddie Quick? Don't seem right, seein' you three without them along."

"They, uh, didn't make it," Chad replied.

"Damn, I'm sorry to hear that," Barry said. "But I read where a lot of good men died out durin' the winter."

Chad, Gene, and Ken looked at each other. They hadn't said anything that would suggest Hank and Eddie died during the winter. And they said nothing to correct Barry's misconception.

"I've got two questions to ask," Chad said. "How do we get that money? And when do we start after them horses?"

Barry pointed to the Border Oasis. "Like I said, you'll prob'ly find Frank Ford or Jim Robison in there. And one or the other of them will have your money. But as for when we start after the horses? Well, I don't reckon that's goin' to happen until after Clay Allison gets here."

Approximately six miles from El Paso, nineteen-year-old Marilou Kincaid walked out to the barn to call her sister and brother in for breakfast. Brenda, her seventeen-year-old sister, was milking, while fifteen-year-old Nate was pitching hay for the animals.

"Breakfast is ready," Marilou said.

"Good," Nate said, resting on the pitchfork. "I'm starving."

"You're always starving," Brenda said.

"At least I'm not so skinny I look like a rope with knots tied in it," Nate teased, tossing some hay at his sister.

"Hey, watch that! You're getting hay in my hair," Brenda complained.

"What are we having?" Nate asked.

"Biscuits, sausage, and gravy. I made the biscuits myself," Marilou said proudly.

"Don't eat the biscuits, Brenda! You'll probably get poisoned," Nate teased.

"You don't have to eat them."

"Oh, I'll eat them, I suppose," Nate said as the three started back up toward the house.

"Now there's a big surprise," Marilou said, and she and Brenda laughed out loud. They were still laughing when Nate pushed the door open, then came to a complete halt, his eyes wide with confusion.

There were three strange men in the kitchen. One was stockily built, with red hair. He was standing behind the children's father. Another was a medium-sized, pale-skinned albino, with eyes so light a pink as to almost be colorless. The albino was holding a knife to their mother's throat.

The third intruder was small, wiry, and dark, with a narrow nose, thin lips, and a jagged purple scar that started just above his left eye, slicing down through it and leaving a puffy mass of flesh, then running down his cheek to hook up under the corner of his mouth. He was standing by the table eating a biscuit-and-sausage sandwich.

"Well, now, would you lookie at these two girls? They'll do fine, just real fine," the scarfaced man said, looking at the two girls with unabashed lust in his eyes.

"I know who you are," Nate said. "I seen your picture on a wanted poster. You're Will Shardeen."

"Boy, you ain't needed," Shardeen growled. He pulled out his gun and, before anyone could say a word, yanked the trigger. The gun roared, a wicked flash of flame jumped from the barrel of the gun and a cloud of smoke billowed out over the table. The bullet hit Nate in the forehead and as he fell back, heavy drops of blood from his wound splattered Brenda's face and hair.

"Nate!" Marilou screamed as her brother fell

to the floor. She dropped to her knees beside him and put her hands on his face, trying desperately to deny what she was seeing.

"Murderers!" Nate's mother yelled. She tried to stand up, but the pale-faced one shoved her back down in her chair, then cut a nick in her face with the tip of his knife. A bright red stream of blood began flowing from the gash.

"Leave her alone!" the father shouted, but his shout was cut off by a blow to the back of his head as the red-haired man brought his gun down sharply.

"What do you want?" Marilou asked. "What are you doing here?"

"What do we want? What does anyone want?" Shardeen asked. "We want money."

"Money? Are you crazy?" the mother replied. "We don't have any. We barely make a living from this place."

Shardeen looked pointedly at Marilou. "Are you a virgin?" he asked.

"What?" Marilou asked, gasping at the impertinence of such a question.

"It's a simple question, girly. Are you a virgin? Have you ever been with a man?"

"That's . . . that's none of your business," Marilou replied.

"Oh, but it is my business. Now I figure your

little sister here is a virgin, for sure," Shardeen said, looking at Brenda. "Seems to me she's too young to be anything else." He looked back at Marilou. "But you're a little older. For all I know, you may of already spread your legs a few times."

"Why . . . why are you concerned, one way or the other?" the girl's mother asked.

Shardeen smiled. "Well, since you asked, there are people in Mexico who are willing to pay a lot of money for Anglo women," he said. "And if they're virgins, why, they'll pay even more."

"You . . . would do such a thing? You would sell young girls to, to people like that?" the mother asked.

"Not just young girls," Shardeen said, putting his hand on the woman's chin and lifting it so he could study her more closely. "Any woman. You'll do, too. I know you're no virgin, but I reckon we'll get enough for you to make it worth our while to take you with us."

"I'm not going with you, and neither are my daughters," the woman said resolutely.

"That's all right by me, lady. If you don't want to go with us, then I don't see no reason for keeping you alive," Shardeen said He cocked his pistol and aimed it at the mother.

"No!" Marilou shouted. "Don't shoot her! She'll go with you! We'll all go with you!"

"Well, now, that's more like it," Shardeen said. He looked over at the other two men with him. "Whitey, you and Red go out to the barn and saddle three horses. Pick out the best ones you can find. Once we get rid of the women, the horses will belong to us."

The albino started toward the door but the stocky one with red hair hung back. Red grabbed himself unabashedly. "Hey, Shardeen, can we have us a little fun with 'em before we sell 'em to the Mexicans?"

"No. We get a hundred dollars more if they are virgins," he said. "I don't aim to give up two hundred dollars just 'cause you can't keep your pecker in your pants. If you want to do somethin', do it with the old woman."

"All right, don't make no never mind to me which one I do it with, anyhow. Just as long as I get to do it," Red replied.

"We ain't got the time till we're down in Mexico. Now get out to the barn and help Whitey with them mounts."

Word of what happened out at the Kincaid Ranch reached town by noon. A neighbor who stopped by discovered the bodies of Hiram Kincaid and his son, Nate. There was no sign of Mrs. Kincaid or the girls.

The sheriff called for a posse and when thirty angry men rode out at about two o'clock that afternoon, it was all Jim, Frank, Barry, Tennessee, Chad, Ken, and Gene could do to keep from going with them.

"You know they aren't going to find anything," Jim told the others, as they stood in front of the saloon and watched the party leave. "They're angry and frustrated and need to do this just to have something to do. But whoever did this is long gone by now."

"I reckon you're right," Barry said. "But if it weren't for the money we already took to do the job, I'd be out there ridin' with them, even though they ain't going to find anybody or anything."

"Let's go have another beer," Tennessee suggested.

When the boys returned to the saloon, they found it nearly empty. Only Jensen, the gambler, had not ridden out with the posse, and he was sitting at a table at the back of the room, dealing hands of poker to himself. Seeing someone come in, Jensen looked up in anticipation of a game, but the smile left his face when he saw that Jim Robison and Frank Ford were with Barry and Tennessee.

Clay Allison arrived about an hour later. He recognized Jim and Frank, and started toward their table with Hector Ortega right behind him.

"Barkeep," Clay called, "bring me a beer, and bring my amigo a tequila."

"I don't have any tequila," Ned said. "If you want something to drink, go to a cantina. That's where the Mexes go," he added, looking pointedly at Ortega. "There's two or three of 'em in town."

"This 'Mex' is staying with us. Bring him a beer, too."

Ned hesitated for a moment, obviously not too pleased with serving a Mexican.

"Boys, this is Clay Allison," Jim said, introducing Clay to the others.

When he mentioned Clay Allison's name, Ned gulped, and his eyes grew wide. He was galvanized into action. He quickly drew two beers, then brought them over to the table.

"Why didn't you say you was with Mr. Allison here? Of course, anyone who is with Mr. Allison is welcome at the Border Oasis anytime, be he Mex or American," the bartender said.

"Where is everyone?" Clay asked, looking around the saloon. "Don't normally see watering holes this quiet, even in the middle of the day."

"Someone murdered a man and his young son at their ranch near here," Jim said. "Nearly the entire town has formed a posse to go after whoever did it."

"Must've been a might popular man to have a posse that large after his killers," Clay said.

"Yeah, well it's not just the murders. The man's wife and daughters are missing, too. The sheriff figures whoever killed the men took the women. Though where he took them, don't nobody have any idea."

"He took them to Mexico," Ortega said in a matter-of-fact manner. He took a swallow of his beer.

"How do you know?"

"The banditos," Ortega said. "They will pay gold for Anglo women."

"So what you are saying is, the women are probably still alive?" Chad asked.

"Sí," Ortega answered. "But it would be better for them if they were not, I think."

Chapter 9

Shardeen, Red, and Whitey were riding hard to the south, down into Old Mexico. Even though Shardeen didn't figure anyone would be following them, he intended to make a wide swing, throwing off anyone who might be tracking them. He looked over at his three captives—the two young girls and their mother. Even though they were mounted on their own horses, there was little chance of their getting away, as the horses were being led and the captives themselves were tied and gagged. They weren't blindfolded, though, and Shardeen enjoyed seeing the terror that was plain on their faces.

Shardeen had given strict orders that neither of the two girls was to be touched because he wanted the extra money they would bring, but he had placed no such restriction on Katie Kincaid, the girls' mother. Because of her age, her value would not be diminished by anything they did.

Actually, Katie was an exceptionally attractive woman, though beauty itself meant absolutely nothing to Shardeen. Whether he was with a young, lovely girl just coming into maturity or an elderly woman dissipated by a lifetime of ordeal and toil made no difference to him. For Shardeen, rape wasn't a sexual experience. It was an exercise in power.

More than the sex itself, Shardeen enjoyed inducing fear in women. He had discovered this particular predilection while riding with a group of vigilantes who sold their services as "Indian Regulators." Anytime there was an Indian disturbance, whether it was one Indian or a group in a war party, the Indian Regulators could sell their services. Hired by those communities too far away from the nearest military outpost to use the regular army, the Indian Regulators would conduct retaliatory raids against the nearest Indian village.

Of course they seldom, if ever, got the Indians who were actually guilty of the crime that had enraged the white settlers, but it didn't matter. The punishment the Regulators inflicted upon the Indians, innocent or not, gave the ranchers, farmers, and citizens of the nearby towns a sense of retaliation. And sometimes it really did have the effect of causing the Indians to police their own a little better.

One of the benefits that Shardeen particularly enjoyed was having his way with captive Indian women. There was no way any court would come after him for raping an Indian woman. The feeling of total domination and control Shardeen enjoyed in such situations was so powerful that he would have ridden with the Indian Regulators whether he was paid or not.

"Hey, Shardeen," Red called up to him, interrupting Shardeen's thoughts. "What do you say we stop for a while? They ain't no way anyone's gonna follow us down here. Besides which, we been travelin' on solid rock for near an hour. They couldn't track us if they was to try."

"Let me take a look-see," Shardeen replied. He halted, then climbed to the top of a pile of huge rocks, holding a collapsed spyglass in his hand. He opened up the telescope and looked back over the way they came. For as far as he could see, he saw nobody. He snapped the glass closed, then came back down from the rocks.

"Did you see anyone?" Red asked.

"No."

"Then we can stop a while?"

"Yeah, all right," Shardeen agreed.

"Good," Red said, getting down from his own horse. He looked toward Katie, then rubbed himself again. "Hey, Shardeen, you said we could have us a little fun with the mama once we was in Mexico, didn't you?"

"That's what I said," Shardeen answered.

Katie shivered involuntarily.

"Well, we're here," he said. Red walked back to Katie Kincaid, then pulled her down from the horse. "Come on, honey. Me an' you's gonna have us a little fun."

Katie's eyes revealed her stark panic and loathing, and she looked at Shardeen as if pleading with him to say something.

"So, Shardeen will you be wantin' a little of the fun after I finish?" Red asked.

"You're askin' the wrong question, Red," Shardeen replied with an evil grin. "What you mean to say is, do I wanna let you have some of the fun after I get finished?"

Not too far away from Shardeen and his captives, Jim, Frank, Barry, Tennessee, Chad, Gene, and Ken were also crossing into northern Mexico. At the moment, they were riding through an area known as the *Cumbres de Majalca*, which,

Hector Ortega explained, meant Summits of Majalca. Though Jim didn't think of it in such terms, the *Cumbres de Majalca* were visually stunning, peppered with high mountains and deep canyons, and strewn with many unique rock formations created by eons of erosion. Ortega had chosen this route because of the readily available water, as there were numerous arroyos sending small winding tributaries through the pine, oak, and dry scrub to the Sacramento and Chuvinca Rivers.

They had been on the trail for four days now, and during that time Hector Ortega had spoken only when it was necessary. At night the short, swarthy Mexican would sit quietly, cleaning the brace of Colt .45s he wore high on his gun belt. By day he rode in silence.

That was all right by Jim and the other Americans, who had no wish to be sociable with him. They had resented the fact that Clay Allison appointed Ortega their trail boss, but there was nothing they could do about it. They had not only accepted half the money, they had already spent much of it, so they had no choice but to go along with Clay Allison's decision.

Jim was thinking about that very thing when, out of the corner of his eye he thought he caught a movement. Just as he was twisting around in his saddle for a closer look, Tennessee slapped his legs against the side of his horse and moved up beside him.

"I make it two men riding alongside us," Tennessee said.

"Yeah, I thought I saw something," Jim answered. "Wonder who they are?"

"Suppose we ask our leader?" Tennessee suggested.

"Good idea," Jim said. He moved up the line. "Ortega," he called.

Ortega looked back at him, but said nothing.

"We're being watched."

Ortega looked around, then shrugged. "I see nothing."

"Look at the notch in the hill off to our left. In just a moment, they'll go through there."

Ortega looked in the direction indicated by Jim, and just as Jim had said, two riders moved quickly through the notch slipping by so expertly that only someone who was specifically looking for them would have noticed.

"Did you see them?" Jim asked.

"Sí."

"Who do you think they are?"

"Perhaps they are *bandidos*."

"*Bandidos?*"

"Sí. There are many *bandidos* in the *Cumbres*

de Majalca. We have come from Texas. Maybe they think we are rich.''

"Well, maybe I had better set them straight," Jim suggested.

Telling the others to continue riding, Jim left the trail and, using a nearby ridgeline for concealment, rode ahead about a thousand yards. He cut over to the gully the two men were following, then dismounted, pulling his Winchester .44-40 from its saddle boot and climbing onto a rocky ledge to wait for them. He jacked a round into the chamber. It would be an easy shot, if he wanted to take it.

He didn't want to kill them, though. He knew there were times when one had to kill, and when those times came, there was no place for hesitancy. He had killed before, and he would kill again when and if it was required. But to the degree he could, he had made a compromise with grim reality: He killed only when he had no other choice. These two riders had not yet put him in such a position.

They really were quite good, Jim thought. They approached so skillfully that he could barely hear them. Not one word was spoken between them, and they guided their horses in a manner that their hooves would barely disturb the loose rock and shale of the gully. Jim watched them come into view around the bend. He stood up suddenly.

"Hijo de puta!" one of the riders exclaimed in a startled shouted. His horse reared, and his hand started toward his pistol.

"Don't do it, *hombre!"* Jim shouted in warning, raising his rifle to his shoulder.

"I would listen to the gringo," the other man said. Both men were wearing large sombreros, colorful serapes, and crossed bandoliers bristling with shells.

"Your amigo is making sense," Jim said.

The one whose hand had started toward his pistol stopped, then got his horse under control.

"I don't know what you hombres are after," Jim said. "But if it's money, you are barking up the wrong tree. We're just out-of-work cowboys."

"We are not *bandidos,* senor," one of the men said.

"I don't give a damn what you are. I'm not taking any chances. I want you both to drop your guns and belts, then turn around and ride out of here."

"Senor, there are many very bad men in this country. It is not safe to be without guns," one of the riders argued.

"You don't say," Jim replied. He made an impatient motion with the barrel of his rifle. "Shuck 'em," he ordered.

Grumbling and protesting their innocence, the two men got rid of their weapons, dropping them onto the rocks with a clatter.

"Now turn your horses around and—" Jim's words were interrupted by two gunshots. Both Mexicans tumbled from their horses.

"What the hell?" Jim shouted, twisting around in his saddle. He saw a wisp of gunsmoke curling up from a rock about twenty-five yards behind him. He raised his own rifle. "Who's there?" he shouted.

Hector Ortega raised up from behind the rock, holding his own rifle over his head.

"It is me, senor! Hector Ortega."

"Ortega! What the hell did you shoot them for?"

Ortega climbed down the side of the large rock until he was just a few feet away from Jim, then he jumped the rest of the way down. "To keep them from shooting you," he said.

"How the hell were they going to shoot me? Their guns were on the ground."

Ortega removed the sombreros from the dead men. Reaching down into the crown of each of the large hats, he pulled out two small pistols. He held the pistols up for Jim's observation.

"They would shoot you with these, I think," he said.

"I'll be damned," Jim replied. "How did you know about those guns?"

"It is a trick many *bandidos* use," Ortega said.

"Well, I reckon I'm beholden to you, Ortega," Jim said, his anger over what he had thought to be senseless killings quickly abating.

Some distance away, a United States marshal and a Texas sheriff were meeting with Capitán Eduardo Bustamante of the Mexican Federales.

"Sí," Bustamante said in answer to one of the American lawmen's question. "We know of Senora Kincaid and the two young senoritas who were captured."

"The thing is, Captain Bustamante," Sheriff Parker said. "We don't believe it was Mexicans who captured 'em. We think it was Americans. But we believe these Americans are going to bring 'em down here and try to sell 'em to one of the bandit gangs in the hills."

"We will be most vigilant," Bustamante promised.

"Does such a thing really happen?" Marshal Gibbons asked. "What I mean is, will the Mexican bandits actually pay for American women?"

"Sí, senor," Bustamante answered. "If they

are young and innocent, they are worth much money in gold."

"Damn. That is the most disgusting thing I have ever heard of," Gibbons said with a sneer. "I mean, how can you Mexicans do such a thing?"

Bustamante flashed Gibbons a look of disdain. "Senor Gibbons, the Mexicans pay money for the unfortunate senoritas—this is true. But it is also true that it is the Americanos who raid the homes, kill the men and capture the senoritas."

"Bustamante is right, Tom," Sheriff Parker said. "We got no right to be throwin' stones down here till we clean up our own house."

"I suppose you're right," Gibbons said. "I apologize, Captain. It's just that, well, I want those girls back safely. Their mama, too, if she is still alive. But what I want more than anything are the American sons of bitches who would do such a thing to their own people."

Bustamante smiled broadly. "Perhaps I will soon have good news for you," he said. "We have learned of a group of Americans traveling south along the Chihuahua Trail."

"You think they might be the ones we are looking for?"

"That we do not know," Bustamante said. "There are no women traveling with them, but we do know that they crossed the border to come into our country at about the same time the women were taken. Perhaps they have left the women somewhere under guard, while they go into the *montañas* to find the evil ones so they can do their business."

"You have reports on such men? Where are they now?" Gibbons asked. "I wouldn't want them to get away."

"Do not worry, senor. They will not get away. The Americans are riding through the *Cumbres de Majalca* now. But Teniente Montoya and Teniente Arino, two of my best men, are keeping a close eye on them."

Chapter 10

It was two days later when Chad saw the poster nailed to a tree. In bold, capital letters at the top of the poster were the words:

MUERTO O VIVO!

Just beneath the words was a line drawing of a man's face. The face was rather round with heavily browed eyes and a large mustache. In truth, the drawing looked like half the Mexicans Chad had seen since they crossed into Mexico. It wasn't the face that attracted Chad's attention, nor the words, none of which Chad could understand. It was the name beneath the picture that Chad saw:

HECTOR ORTEGA
DESEADO PARA ASESINATO
DIEZ MIL RECOMPENSES DEL PESO.
POLICIA FEDERAL MEJICANO DEL CONTACTO

Chad removed the poster. That night, when they made camp, he showed it to Jim.

"What do you think this means?"

"I don't know," Jim said. He studied it for a moment, then said, "From the way it's put together, I'd say it is a wanted poster. Look at the bottom line, poli . . . polisee-ah," he struggled with the word, then said, "*Policia*. Police. Federal police. And this last word: *contacto*. Contact, you think?"

"*Mejicano*," Chad said, "must mean Mexican."

"Contact the Mexican Federal Police," Jim said.

The others, made curious by Jim and Chad's secretive conversation, came over to see what was going on.

"What you boys ponderin' over?" Barry asked.

"Chad found this today," Jim said, showing him the poster.

"What the hell?" Tennessee asked. "You think that's our Ortega?"

"Ours? You ready to claim him now?" Ken asked.

The others laughed.

"You know what I mean," Ken said, a little miffed at being teased.

"You have to admit, it does look a little like him," Gene said.

"Yeah, looks like him, and like every Mexican we've come across since we came down into this godforsaken land," Gene insisted.

"Well, there's no gettin' around one thing, and that is the fact that the fella on this poster is named Hector Ortega, and so is our trail boss. And the drawing of this Hector Ortega looks a lot like the man we're trailin' with," Tennessee said. "So I figure it's something we ought to find out about."

Ortega, who was at that moment eating from a can of beans, realized that the others were engaged in some sort of discussion. He had no idea what the subject of the conversation was, but knew it must be about him because he heard his name, and they kept looking over toward him.

"Senors," he finally asked, "what are you doing?"

"Are you goin' to tell him?" Ken asked.

"Tell him?" Jim replied. He shook his head. "I'm not going to tell him a damn thing, because I don't know what to tell him. I reckon I'll just have to come right out and ask him."

Jim took the paper over to Ortega and showed it to him.

"Have you seen this?"

"Sí." Ortega ate another spoonful of beans before he spoke again, answering in a very nonchalant voice. "Many times I have seen this poster."

"Is this supposed to be a picture of you?" Jim pointed to the drawing.

Ortega rubbed his hand across his cheek. "I do not think it looks very much like me," he said.

"The name on the poster is Hector Ortega. That is your name, isn't it?"

"Sí, that is my name. But it is also the name of many of my people. In Mexico the name Hector Ortega is like the name Bill Smith in America. There are many, many people with that name."

Jim studied the line drawing for a moment longer, then he looked very closely at Ortega. Finally he shook his head. "I guess you're right. But tell me what the words say."

"Dead or alive," Ortega said, indicating the large words at the top. "The name, Hector Ortega, you have already read. The other words read, 'Wanted for murder. Ten thousand peso reward. Contact the federal police.' "

"Yes, the part about contact the federal police part we figured out for ourselves," Jim said.

The other Americans had drifted over as well to listen to Ortega's translation.

"You say this isn't you," Barry began. "Do you know who this other fella with your name is?"

Ortega shook his head. "It could be anyone," he said. He smiled. "Perhaps one of the *bandidos* we killed yesterday is the man in this poster. If so, we are ten thousand pesos richer today."

"Not we, *you*," Jim said. "You are the one who killed those men. I wanted no part of it then, and I want no part of it now."

Ever since dark, Katie Kincaid had been working diligently to untie her hands. It was a difficult task, not only because Whitey, who had tied Katie and her two daughters, was good with rope but also because she had to be very still and quiet lest she give away what she was doing. By the time she finally managed to get her hands free, she estimated that it was a little after midnight. Even though her hands were now free, she kept her wrists crossed on top of her body so that it would appear to the casual observer in the dark that she was still securely tied.

She could hear the troubled but even breathing of her two daughters, so she knew they were both sleeping. By the loud snoring coming from the other side of the small clearing, she could tell that Shardeen and Whitey were fast asleep as well. It was Red's time to be on guard. Several minutes earlier she had overheard Red coming on guard, and Shardeen going off.

"You stay awake. Keep the fire goin', and keep a close eye on them women," Shardeen had ordered.

"You don't have to worry none about me," Red replied.

"And stay the hell away from 'em," Shardeen ordered.

"I ain't goin' to bother the girls none." Red rubbed himself, then looked toward the three slumbering women.

"I ain't talkin' about just the girls. I mean I want you to stay away from their mama, too," Shardeen said. "I'm tired, and I don't want my sleep ruined by listening to you grunt and her squeal."

"Two, three more times and 'bout the only squealin' she'll be doin' is when she's tellin' me how much she's likin' it," Red bragged.

"Mind what I say," Shardeen said. "I don't want to get woke up."

"Go on, then. Go to sleep and quit gabbin' about it."

When, a moment later, Red came over to look at the three captives, Katie made no movement nor uttered any sound that would suggest she was awake. She had her eyes nearly closed, so much so that in the flickering yellow light of the campfire, Red couldn't tell that she was actually looking at him through narrowed slits. Satisfied that all were asleep, Red gathered several sticks of dry wood and fed the campfire. The burning wood began to pop and snap as the flames grew larger. The bubble of golden light and warmth extended farther from the fire.

If Katie was ever going to make good her plan to escape, now was the time to put it into operation. Her plan depended upon two things: being able to get her hands free, and finding the opportunity to get Red alone. Just as he was, right now.

Red was perfect for her plan, because out of their three captors, he was the one who seemed most driven by primordial instincts. He was constantly badgering Shardeen to take a break for food or the toilet, and to allow him to gratify himself sexually with Katie. And while after the first couple of times Whitey and Shardeen's sexual appetites were reduced, Red was as eager now as he had been when the women were first captured.

Red was also the slowest of wit. Shardeen and Whitey were constantly explaining the most basic things to him.

The third and final reason was the fact that Red used a cross draw. He wore his pistol on the left side of his gun belt, with the handle facing forward. That was an important element in Katie's plan.

"Red?" Katie whispered in the dark.

"What? Who's there?" Red replied.

"Shhh," Katie said. "Do you want to wake Shardeen?"

Red got up from the rock and walked over to look down at her. "What do you want?" he asked.

"Shhh!" Katie said again. "Speak softly, Red," she said. "Whisper. Otherwise you'll wake the others and we can't have our fun."

"Fun?"

"Do you think you are the only one who enjoys it when we have sex?"

A shocked expression lighted up Red's face. Then he turned toward his two sleeping partners. He held up his finger as if making a point. "Damnation! I told Shardeen . . ." Red started to say out loud.

"Shhh! You must whisper."

"I told Shardeen you was goin' to come around to likin' it," Red whispered lasciviously.

"Oh, honey, I liked it the first time," Katie said.

"You sure didn't act like it."

"I had to pretend. I didn't want my daughters to know how much I liked it," Katie said. "They wouldn't understand. They are too young to know how good it can be when you are with a real man. Someone like you, I mean."

"I'll be damned. I knowed it was somethin' like that." Red began rubbing himself flagrantly now.

"Oh, you don't have to play with yourself, Red. We could have some fun right now, just the two of us," Katie said. "And if we are quiet about it, nobody would ever have to know. Not my two daughters, not Whitey, and especially not Shardeen."

"Yeah," Red said, smiling. He started toward her, then he stopped and looked at her suspiciously, as if he suspected she might be trying something sly. "I ain't goin' to untie you," he said.

"All right, you don't have to untie me. But you will pull up my skirt and pull down my drawers, won't you? As long as my hands are tied, I can't do it myself."

"Yeah," Red repeated. "I sure will pull up your skirt and pull down your drawers."

Kneeling beside her, Red helped her undress, pulling her clothes down below her knees. Her naked white flesh gleamed softly in the moonlight.

"Oh, honey, I'm no fire for you," Kate moaned in a low, throaty voice.

"Yeah, yeah," Red said. He was breathing in ragged gasps as he began to move over her.

"Wait, aren't you going to untie my ankles?"

"Why should I do that?"

"Oh, honey, believe me, it will be so much better for you if you will untie my ankles. It will let me spread my legs wider for you. You do want me to spread my legs for you, don't you?"

"Yeah, spread your legs," Red grunted, as he bent down to untie her ankles.

"Hurry, don't keep me waiting for you any longer," Katie said, spreading her legs in invitation once her ankles were untied.

Red knelt between Katie's wide-spread legs. Then he unbuttoned his pants and started to mount her. At that moment Katie slipped her hand from the loose coil of rope that was around her wrists, wrapped her fingers around the handle of Red's pistol, slipped it from his holster, shoved the barrel of the gun into his belly and pulled the trigger.

Red's body muffled the gunshot, so instead of

a loud bang, it was more like the pop of a log in the fire. But the shot itself propelled Red off Katie so she was able to sit up.

"Mama?" Marilou said.

"Shhh!" Katie said. "Be quiet." Pulling her drawers up and her skirt down, Katie moved over to Marilou and began untying her, all the while keeping an eye on the still-sleeping forms of Whitey and Shardeen.

Marilou untied her own ankles as Katie began untying Brenda's hands.

Once Brenda's hands were free the girls, cautioned by Katie to be as silent as possible, worked quickly and quietly to get their own horses saddled.

Once the three horses were saddled, Katie walked back over to Red's body. Leaning over him, she undid his gun belt and slipped it off his waist. Both Marilou and Brenda thought she was going to keep it. Instead, she dropped it into the fire. Then she hurried back to her horse.

"Get mounted," she said quietly. "But just walk them slowly for now. When the excitement starts, ride as fast as you can."

"What excitement, Mama?" Brenda asked.

"You'll see," Katie promised.

The three women started riding slowly and quietly out of the camp. They were about fifty yards away when the cartridges in Red's gunbelt started going off, activated by the heat of the campfire.

It sounded as if an army had invaded, with the shots occurring so rapidly as to be on top of each other. Looking back toward the camp, the three women could see sparks flying from the fire. They could also see Shardeen and Whitey rolling around on the ground, with their arms covering their heads.

"Ahh! What the hell! We surrender! We surrender!" Shardeen shouted.

The outlaws' three unsaddled horses soon came galloping by the women. The horses, whinnying loudly with flared nostrils, had been terrified by the sudden and unexpected noise in the middle of the night. Katie knew they would run for miles before calming down. Shardeen and Whitey would be left afoot, deep in the mountains of northern Mexico.

Over the last few days, Katie had seen her husband and son murdered. She had been raped, she'd watched fear grow in the eyes of her two young daughters, and she had just been forced to kill another human being. If someone had told her one week ago that she would have to endure such an ordeal, she would not have believed herself capable of surviving.

But she had survived. And now, with bullets popping, Shardeen and Whitey screaming in fear, and the outlaws' horses galloping off into the night, she was actually able to enjoy one of the best laughs of her entire life.

Chapter 11

In the churchyard of the Mexican town of Chihuahua, Father Sanchez began the funeral prayer of commitment as two women stepped up to the open graves and dropped dirt onto the coffins of the dead. The women, the widows of the two slain policemen, were dressed in black with their faces covered by veils.

Capitán Bustamante stood a little way behind the mourners, holding his hat in his hand as the funeral ended. As the two widows were leaving the graveyard, he stepped out to confront them.

"Senoras," he said in a solemn voice, "this, I promise you: The men who murdered your husbands will pay for this crime with their own blood."

The older of the two women, Senora Montoya,

stopped and looked at Bustamante through eyes that were bloodshot and red-rimmed from crying. For a long, uncomfortable moment, she held him with her stare. Finally, in a low, woeful voice, she spoke.

"And when these men are dead, Capitán, will our husbands be returned to us?" she asked.

Bustamante blinked his eyes a few times, surprised by the woman's response.

"No, and for that I am sorry."

"Then do not speak to me of murderers paying in blood. Their lives will bring me no comfort. Not if it does not bring my husband back to me," Senora Montoya insisted.

Father Sanchez hurried over to comfort the two widows. He flashed Bustamante an admonishing glance. "My son, do not speak of more killing in this holy place," he said.

Bustamante left the churchyard. Behind him in the church belfry, a muffled bell tolled once for each year lived by the two slain policemen, thirty-two times for Montoya, twenty-eight for Arino. The bell tolls could be heard all over the town, and when Bustamante walked through the plaza, he saw that many were standing with their hats held reverently across their chests as they waited for the funeral to end.

The tolling didn't cease until Bustamante was

in his office. He hung his sombrero on a peg, then glanced over at his deputy, Lieutenant, or Teniente, Santos.

"How was the funeral?" Santos asked.

"Very sad."

From outside, they could hear the hoofbeats of a galloping horse.

"Someone is in a great hurry," Bustamante said.

"Listen, someone is shouting," Santos said.

"Senor Capitán! Senor Capitán!"

Bustamante looked through the front window of the office. "It is Jose Meras."

The rider stopped in front of the police station then swung down from the saddle, just as Bustamante and Santos came outside to see what it was about.

"Capitán Bustamante, the men who killed Montoya and Arino," Meras shouted excitedly. "It was seven gringos and one Mexican. They have been seen!"

"Where?"

"In the mountains, near the village of Escalon."

"Escalon?" Bustamante turned to Santos. "Teniente Santos, who is in charge of the police at Escalon?" he asked.

"Sargento Gonzales."

"Only a sargento? No officers?"

"It is a very small station, senor," Santos replied.

"Very well. I will send a telegram to Sargento Gonzales, telling him that these men may be coming to his village."

"Gonzales has but one man assigned to him, Capitán," Santos said. "I do not think he can arrest eight men."

"All the better. I will tell him to take no action, but just to observe them until we get there. After all, why give the glory to a mere sargento, when, by rights, it should be ours to claim. Santos, call the company together," Bustamante ordered. "We are going after the murderers."

"Sí, senor! Why give the credit to a mere sargento?" Santos replied with a big smile on his face.

Chickens squawked and scurried to get out of the way as Jim Robison and his friends followed Hector Ortega across the plaza of the little village of Escalon. A couple of men who were lazing in the shade, their sombreros shielding their eyes, made no effort to move as the riders passed within a few feet of them. An old woman was drawing water in the middle of the plaza and Jim and the others rode over to the well and dismounted. Without having to ask for it, the old woman offered her dipper to them.

"Gracias," Jim said, taking the dipper. He drank deeply, then passed the dipper over to the others. Only Ortega didn't drink from the well. Instead, he sat in his saddle in silence, watching the others.

"I know the son of a bitch don't talk," Tennessee said. "But don't he drink water?"

"Mujer, trae agua," Ortega said to the old woman at the well.

"Sí, senor," the old woman replied. Filling the dipper with water, she carried it over to Ortega and handed it up to him.

Ortega drank thirstily.

"Maybe the son of a bitch thinks he is too good to get his own water," Tennessee said.

Ortega tossed away the remaining few drops, then handed the dipper back to the old woman. He looked directly at Tennessee.

"I am your chief," he said. "It would not look good in the eyes of my people if I drank at the well with those who are beneath me."

"Beneath you? What do you mean, beneath you? I'll show you who is—" Tennessee spouted angrily, but Jim put out his hand to stop him.

"Easy there, Tennessee," Jim said.

"Easy? You just going to let him talk like that?"

"Yes."

"Senor, I suggest you listen to your friend," Ortega said to Tennessee. "He is man who knows his place."

"You son of a bitch! I wish I knew enough Spanish to cuss you out in your own language," Tennessee sputtered.

Again, Jim interrupted him. "That's enough, Tennessee. Remember, he is our trail boss."

"That's right," Ortega said with a broad smile. "I am your *jefe*."

"Jim, I've never knowed you to show the white feather like that," Tennessee said.

"I've got my reasons," Jim said.

"I hope so."

"I must go somewhere for a few days," Ortega said. "Stay here until I return."

"Are you going after the horses?" Jim asked.

"Sí. I go after the horses." Ortega pointed across the plaza. "There is a hotel behind the cantina. Wait there."

"What will we do about our own horses?" Tennessee asked.

"There is a place over there for your horses as well. I will be back in three days." Without so much as a nod, Ortega rode off.

"So, Jim, you want to tell us why you was givin' in to that bastard?" Barry asked.

"We've come all the way down here to get a herd of horses and take them back up to Colorado. Do any of you know where we are supposed to get these horses?" Jim asked.

"No."

'No, and neither do I. Ortega is the only one who does know. And since that's why we came down here in the first place, and since we don't get the rest of our money until we take them back, I plan to let that son of a bitch have his way on everything. After we get the horses, it'll be a different matter."

"Why? What do you plan to do then?"

Jim smiled at the others. "Why, I reckon Senor Ortega is goin' to have to tangle with the surliest bunch of wranglers anyone ever run across. In the meantime, we'll just take it easy here, like he said."

"Take it easy? How can you take it easy in a flyblown dump like this? What are we supposed to do for the next few days?"

"Any of you boys ever developed a likin' for tequila?"

"I've drunk it," Tennessee said, screwing up his nose in distaste. "But it sure don't hold a candle to Tennessee sour mash."

"Or Kentucky bourbon," Ken added.

"Well, I've run across a few folks back in the States who really like it," Jim said. "They say you have to take it with salt and lemon, but once you learn how to do it, it's pretty good."

"Yeah, well, whatever it is, it has to be better than nothin' to drink at all," Gene said. "And if we really have three days here, I reckon we have the time to learn to like it."

"What do you say we get our lessons started now?" Jim suggested. "Then after that . . ." he let the sentence hang.

"After that, what?" Tennessee asked.

"I don't know if you've noticed, but some of the senoritas are really pretty," Jim said. "And they say that with enough tequila, all of them are beautiful."

"Then what are we standing around out here for? Let's get started," Ken suggested.

The others laughed.

On the other side of the plaza from the cantina, unnoticed by the Americans, was the office of the Mexican Federal Police.

Sargento Gonzales was holding a telegram he had recently received from the district headquarters in Chihuahua, advising him to be on the lookout for a group of white murderers who had crossed the border into Mexico. He stood at the window of his office and looked toward the well, where the seven Americans were drinking water. The eighth man, a Mexican, did not dismount, but drank from the dipper handed him by an old woman who was at the well.

Gonzales reread the wire that had been sent.

> *Tenientes Arino and Montoya were murdered by seven Americans who are riding with one Mexican. Before leaving Texas, the Americans are believed to have murdered a man named Kincaid and his son, both citizens of the United States. After murdering the Kincaid men, the outlaws stole Senora Kincaid and her two daughters, transporting them across the border to Mexico.*
>
> *You are ordered to be especially vigilant but to take no direct action should these desperados arrive in your village.*

Carefully, Gonzales counted the Americans. There were seven of them. And the Mexican on horseback made up the eighth man. The numbers and makeup of the band coincided exactly with the information contained in the wire.

"Diputado Reyna, they are here," Gonzales said from the window.

Reyna, the deputy, who was polishing the chimney of an oil lantern, looked up at his chief.

"Sí," he replied. He started to go back to the polishing, then he looked up again. "Who is here, Sargento?"

"The gringos who murdered Tenientes Arino and Montoya. They are here, in the plaza, right now."

Setting the lamp down carefully, Reyna moved quickly over to the window. He counted the men in the plaza. "There are seven of them," he said. "Eight, if you count the Mexican."

"Sí. That is why I know they are who they are. Montoya and Arino were murdered by seven gringos, riding with one Mexican."

Gonzales looked at Reyna as a huge smile spread across the sergeant's porcine face. "Reyna, do you know what this means? All of Mexico is looking for them and they have come here, to Escalon. What an opportunity! The telegram from Chihuahua says we are to take no actin. But they are here and I will not let them get away."

"There are seven of them," Reyna warned again.

"Sí, seven."

"Senor Sargento, did you not also say the wire from Chihuahua says we are to take no action?" Reyna asked.

Gonzales's eyes shined brightly as he looked

at Reyna. "Do you know how fortunate we are that they have come to our village? After we capture them, the reward will be great. I will be a teniente and you, Diputado Reyna, will be a sargento."

"But there are only two of us!"

"We will have men from the town help us," Gonzales said."

"Men from town? They are peasants. Why do you think they will help us?"

"They will do it because they love their country. They will do it because I will ask them to do it. And they will do it because the government will give fifty pesos to each man who helps."

"The Mexican is riding away," Reyna said, watching the plaza.

"Let him go. He is of no consequence to us. Look, the gringos are going to the cantina. Quickly, Reyna, gather the others. On this day we will make history!"

With a look of trepidation, Reyna left the office to do the bidding of his chief.

"No, no, you gotta do it like this," Jim explained. He licked salt from the back of his wrist, took a bite from the cut lemon, then swallowed some tequila.

"Let me try," Ken said. He took a swallow of tequila, then tried to lick the salt off his wrist. But he had not yet swallowed the tequila, and when he opened his mouth to lick the salt, he wound up spewing tequila all over the place.

The others laughed,. "Hey, dummy, hasn't anyone ever told you that you should never open your mouth when it is full of hooch?" Gene asked.

The others guffawed again.

"Well, what we need is another couple of lemons," Tennessee said. "Amigo," he called to the bartender. When the bartender didn't answer, Tennessee looked down toward the other end of the bar. "That's funny," he said.

"What's funny?" Jim asked. He had just sprinkled his wrist with salt and was getting ready to take another lick.

"The barkeep is gone," Tennessee said.

"Not only the barkeep," Chad added. "Look around the place. Weren't there some folks in here when we came in a few minutes ago?"

"Yes, there were," Jim answered, looking around in surprise.

"Yeah, well, except for us, this place is totally empty," Chad said.

"Where the hell did everybody go?" Frank asked.

"I know we been on the trail a while, but I

didn't know we smelled that bad," Tennessee teased.

For a second, Jim was as confused as everyone else. Then a sudden awareness of danger pricked him.

"Holy shit!" he shouted at the top of his voice. "Everyone get down!"

Almost on top of Jim's shout, gunfire erupted from out in the plaza. A fusillade of bullets smashed through the windows and crashed into the mirror behind the bar. Several bottles of liquor shattered as well. Even as the shooting continued from outside, the boys could hear the gurgling of the rotgut and tequila pouring out of them.

Jim turned over a table and the others did the same thing. They moved three of the tables together, making a barricade.

"Who is out there?" Tennessee asked.

"If you ask me, it's the whole town," Chad replied.

"Why are they shooting at us? We haven't done anything!" Tennessee said. "I'm going to tell them it is a mistake!"

Rising up from behind the table, Tennessee started toward the front door.

"Tennessee, you fool! Get back here!" Jim shouted.

Jim's warning went unheeded and Tennessee

took two steps toward the front door, his hand raised chest-high. Then he was hit. Putting his hand to his chest, Tennessee spun around with a surprised look on his face and with blood spilling through his fingers.

"Barry?" he said in a strained voice. He tried to return to the tables, then pitched forward, falling facedown.

"Tennessee!" Barry shouted, crawling toward the man he had ridden and bunked with for the last three years.

"How is he?" Jim called over the sound of snapping gunfire and whistling, crashing bullets.

"He's dead!" Barry replied.

"Jim, what are we going to do?" Frank asked.

"We've got to get out of here," Jim said. He looked toward the back door. "All the shooting is coming from the front, so we'll go through the back. That's where our horses are, anyway!"

"We'll never make it to the back door," Chad warned. "You saw what happened to Tennessee."

"Pull the tables along with us. We'll crawl across the floor, using the tables as shields until we reach the back door."

"Well, if we're goin' to do it, let's git!" Frank said. "It's getting' hot as hell in here!"

As the bullets continued to whip by them, banging into the tabletops but not punching through the thick wood, the men crawled low across the cantina floor. They reached the back door without anyone else being hurt.

"All right, we're here! Let's go!" Ken shouted. He stood up and kicked open the back door. As he did so, he saw a Mexican standing just outside the door, holding a double-barreled shotgun. The Mexican pulled the triggers and both barrels discharged in a loud roar. With a gaping hole in his chest, Ken was hurled back into the room.

The Mexican killed Ken at the cost of his own life, for all five survivors fired simultaneously. The Mexican went down, riddled with bullets.

Frank went out first, followed by the others. Jim was the last one out. Amazingly, except for the one man with the shotgun, no one else was waiting out back for them.

As soon as they mounted they saw the next problem facing them. The area between the cantina and the hotel was actually an enclosed courtyard with only one exit. That single avenue was along the north side of the cantina, opening out onto the plaza. In order to reach one of the roads leading out of town, they would have to ride right through the middle of that plaza. That was going to be extremely difficult for, at present, the plaza was brimming with nearly two dozen armed men.

"Look where this leads to! It opens right onto the plaza. What'll we do now?" Chad called.

"Barry, you and Gene get Tennessee and Ken out here," Jim ordered.

"What?"

"Hurry! Get them out here."

"What are you talking about, Jim? They're dead!" Gene shouted.

"Do you think I don't know they're dead! That's why what I have in mind can't hurt them," Jim said. "Just do what I say! Chad, you and Frank watch the side in case anyone starts back here."

Almost as soon as he spoke, four Mexicans started running along the side of the cantina. Chad and Frank cut two of them down, and the other two turned and ran back to the front.

Barry and Gene returned inside the cantina they had just evacuated. A moment later they reappeared, pulling the bodies of their two dead friends behind them.

"Put them up on their horses," Jim ordered. "Not belly down. Sitting up."

"How the hell are we going to make them set up?" Gene asked.

"Figure out a way, dammit!" Jim shouted as

he fired at two Mexicans who had moved from the corner of the adjacent building to try to get a better firing position. Though he didn't hit them, his bullets did come close enough to dissuade them from their attempt.

"Use their rifles," Chad suggested. "Stick the rifles down the back of their shirt to hold them upright. Then tie their bodies into the saddle with rope."

"Good idea!" Jim said. "But hurry!"

It took but a moment to have Ken and Tennessee sitting upright, or nearly so, in their saddles. When Jim looked at them and saw their ashen, lifeless faces, he felt a great sadness and a twinge of regret for the way he was about to use the bodies of his friends.

"Boys, wherever you are, if you can see what's going on here and help us out, we can sure use it," Jim said praying to their departed spirits.

The horses were a little skittish and hard to control. They smelled death, and it was obvious they weren't eager to accept the burden of carrying riders who were dead. The animals wanted to bolt, and Jim hoped that their skittishness would work to his advantage.

"What are you aimin' to do with them fellas?" Gene asked.

"Get mounted," Jim said. "I'm going to send

Ken and Tennessee out first. When they get everyone's attention, we'll go, but not until then."

"Which way will we go?" Gene asked.

"Watch Ken and Tennessee. Whichever way their horses break, we'll go in the opposite direction," Jim explained. "Now get ready!"

A slap on the two horses' flanks sent them galloping out into the square. Just as Jim had hoped, the galloping horses and their grisly riders caught the attention of the men in the plaza. The two horses bolted toward the north, and at least two dozen men from the plaza ran after them, firing as they ran. Jim saw dust fly up from the backs of both Tennessee and Ken as several bullets found their mark. Even though he knew they were already dead, he couldn't help but wince for them.

"Now!" Jim shouted.

Slapping his legs against the sides of his horse, he started south. The others followed him and were halfway across the plaza before Gonzales or any of his impromptu deputies realized they had been tricked. Turning, the posse opened fire on the five escaping gringos.

Jim bent low over the neck of his horse, riding hard. Hot air seared his lungs as he drew in great, ragged gulps. His chest pounded and his skin tingled because he expected a bullet in his back at any moment.

Although none of the citizens of Escalon were mounted, Jim held his little group at a gallop for at least five minutes before he felt they were out of immediate danger. Then, holding up his hand, he signaled the others to stop. As they sat there, he could hear them, man and horse, gasping hard for breath.

"Son of a bitch!" Gene shouted. "We made it!'

"I don't think that all of us made it," Chad said, speaking in a small, pained voice.

Struck by the tone in the young man's voice, Jim looked toward him. "Chad, you're wounded?"

"Yes."

"How bad?"

"Pretty bad," Chad said. With that, he fell from his saddle. It was almost as if he had been holding on by sheer willpower until this moment. Now, with the immediate danger over, he let go of that will, and when he did, there was nothing left to sustain him.

Jim jumped from his saddle and hurried over to his young friend. "Chad, take it easy," he said. "We'll rest here a while."

Chad forced a laugh. "Jim, looks like I'm going to be resting here from now on," he said. "Funny, I never thought I'd wind up buried down here in ol' Mexico." He closed his eyes.

"Chad? Chad?" Jim called to him.

"How is he?" Barry asked. "How bad is he hurt?"

Jim felt for a pulse, then leaned over and put his ear to Chad's chest. He listened for a long moment. Then he straightened up, sighed, and shook his head.

"He's dead," he said.

Chapter 12

"Mama, I'm hungry," Brenda said.

"I know, sweetheart," Katie answered. "We're all hungry, but there's nothing we can do about it except just keep on."

"Do you have any idea where we are?" Marilou asked.

Katie twisted around in her saddle and looked toward the sun. "Well, it's still morning, and the sun is off to our right," she said. "That means we're going north. And if we keep going north long enough, we're bound to get back home."

The three women rode on in silence for several more minutes. Then Katie held up her hand. "Stop," she said, quietly.

"What is it, Mama?" Marilou asked.

Kate swung down from the saddle and, holding the pistol before her, started walking toward a bush. There, in the bush, hungrily cropping leaves, was a young wild goat.

"Oh, Mama, look," Brenda said. "He's so cute."

"Not cute, honey, delicious," Katie said. "That's our lunch."

When Jim, Frank, Barry, and Gene heard the gunshot, Jim held up his hand to stop the others.

"Where did it come from?" Barry asked.

"Over there, on the other side of that little ridge, I think," Gene answered.

"Frank, hold the horses," Jim ordered. "Barry, Gene, come with me."

With pistols in hand, Jim, Barry, and Gene dismounted, moved at a crouch toward the ridge, then slipped up to the crest.

"Mama, you got it!" they heard a female voice say in English.

Jim looked over the rise of the hill and saw three women moving toward a goat. Though hit, the goat was still twitching.

"He's not dead," one of the girls said.

"Get a stick," the older of the three said. "I'll finish killing him."

"Oh, Mama, are you going to hit him? Wouldn't it be more humane to shoot him again?"

"I don't want to waste any more bullets," the

older of the three women said. "If Shardeen and Whitey come after us, we may need them."

"I have a knife," Jim offered, standing suddenly and starting down the hill toward the three women. "I'll finish him off for you."

The older of the three women swung her pistol around toward Jim and cocked it.

"Who are you?" she asked.

"The name is Jim Robison, ma'am. And like you, I'm an American."

"What are you doing here?"

"My pards and I have come down here to get a herd of horses. The question is, what are *you* three doing here?"

"Believe me, we aren't here by choice. What do you mean, your partners?"

"They're up there," Jim said, nodding toward the crest of the ridgeline. "Why don't you lower that hog leg, and I'll have them come on down?"

Katie thought about it for a moment, then, with a sigh, lowered her pistol. If they really did have her covered, it would be suicide for her daughters and her if she tried anything now. Besides, whoever they were, they weren't Shardeen and Whitey.

"My name is Katie Kincaid," she said. "These are my two daughters, Marilou and Brenda."

Jim turned toward the ridge. "Gene, Barry, get Frank and you boys come on down," he called out. After that, he started toward the still-twitching goat. Using his knife, he made a quick cut of the jugular vein. The goat bled profusely for a moment then stopped twitching.

"I'll get some wood for a fire," Barry offered.

"I haven't invited you to join us," Katie said.

"No, ma'am, you haven't," Jim replied. "But it seems to me like there might be enough here to feed all of us. That is, if you don't mind a little company."

Katie thought about it for a moment

"Mama, if Shardeen and Whitey show up, it might be good to have someone around," Marilou said.

Jim was in the process of skinning the goat, and when he heard Marilou say Shardeen's name, he looked up quickly.

"Did you say Shardeen?"

"Yes," Katie answered. "Is this man Shardeen a friend of yours?"

Jim shook his head. "I'd hardly call him a friend," he said, "though I have made his acquaintance Why would he be showing up?"

"He captured us," Katie said.

"Captured you?"

"He came to our ranch, killed my husband

and son, then took the three of us captive. He was going to sell us."

"What do you mean, sell you?" Barry asked, surprised by the comment. "Sell you to do what?"

Katie just stared at him.

Then, realizing what she meant, Barry said, "Oh," blushing profusely.

"We are trying to get back home to Texas," Katie said. "'If you will help us, if you will be our protection, I'll pay you. I can't pay you until we get back, of course, because I have no money with me. But I will pay you what I can when we get back home."

"Right now, it's all we can do to protect ourselves," Jim said. "We just lost three of our number."

"Lost? Lost how?"

"I mean we just had three of our friends shot and killed," Jim explained.

"By who? Who is after you?"

"As nearly as I can tell, the Federales are after us."

"The Mexican police? Why? What have you done?"

"That's just it. We ain't done nothin'," Gene said.

"The police don't come after you for no reason at all. Not even the Mexican police," Katie said.

"Until this moment, I had no idea why they were after us," Jim said. "But after what you just told us, I think I'm beginning to see. I believe they came after us thinking we was the ones that killed your man and your boy."

Katie ran her hand through her hair, then nodded. "That might be the case," she said. "If so, I'm sorry you got caught up in our troubles. Especially your friends who were killed. But I must say I'm glad someone knows about us and is trying to do something, even if they are after the wrong men."

"Yes, ma'am, I reckon I can see your point," Jim said as he finished skinning the goat. "I just wish they'd been a mite more sure before they started shootin' at us, is all."

By now Barry had a fire roaring. Jim rose from his task.

"Well, he's skinned and gutted, and there's a fire goin' so you can cook him. But goat's no good without salt. I've got plenty of that. What do you say? Are we sharing?"

Katie nodded. "We're sharing," she said.

It took the goat a couple of hours to cook, though it had been cut into smaller pieces. The aroma was doubly enticing to the exceptionally hungry people, and even before it cooled, they began eating hot pieces of the meat, tossing the meat from hand to hand, blowing and nibbling at it.

Katie studied the men. Jim, the oldest, was about her age. The other three were younger, much closer to the age of her two daughters. Though she believed that she and her daughters might have been better off had they avoided any contact with men at all, she didn't think that this bunch represented any danger to her. And they were American. That helped. Finally she came to a decision.

"Me and my girls will just tag along with you, if you don't mind," she said.

"I told you, ma'am, we aren't going back to Texas. Leastwise, not till we get them horses," Jim replied.

"What's so all-fired important about getting those horses?"

"We've been paid half the money for a job," Jim said. "We won't get the other half until we deliver the horses. I want that money."

"Yes, I can understand that. But I am willing to pay you an amount equal to what you would get if you delivered the horses."

"I appreciate that, ma'am, but I don't hold with takin' pay for something I don't do. We've already drawn the first half of our pay on the promise that we would deliver the horses, and that's what I aim to do."

Katie nodded. "I admire you for that, Mr. Robison," she said. "Where are the horses?"

"In Durango."

"You say you just lost three of your men?"

"Yes, ma'am. Like I said, we got involved in a shootout back in Escalon. Tennessee, Ken, and Chad were killed."

"Then I reckon that makes you short by three wranglers," Katie said. "If I can't pay you one way, I'll pay you another. We'll be your extra wranglers."

"You're women," Frank said with a sniggering laugh.

"Wrangling is hard work," Jim replied in a nicer tone.

"We may be women but we are ranchin' women," Katie replied. "Believe me, we are no strangers to hard work."

"Why would you even want to do such a thing?" he asked.

"Because I'm not sure I can I can get us back to Texas without help. Also, there is safety in numbers. Not only against Shardeen, but against anyone else who might try something."

"Mama," Brenda said, apprehensively, "how do you know these men are safe?"

"Honey, anyone who intends to wrangle a herd of horses all the way back to Texas is too dumb to be dangerous," Katie said matter-of-factly.

Jim laughed. "All right, ma'am," he finally said after he finished laughing. "You and your two daughters are welcome to come along."

Chapter 13

When Hector Ortega returned to the little town of Escalon, it was abuzz with excitement. There were seven bodies lying in the square. Four of the bodies were Mexican, including Gonzales's *diputado*, Juan Reyna. The slain deputy and villagers were being mourned by Reyna's wife, the widows of the other slain villagers, as well as several black-shawled women.

The other three bodies, separated from the Mexicans by some twenty yards, were Americans. Two of the Americans had been killed during the battle in town. The third was found about five miles away. He had been badly wounded as he rode away and had apparently died on the trail. No one was weeping for the

Americans, though several dozen of the villagers were gathered around them, drawn by a gruesome curiosity.

The village padre had been comforting the widows of the slain. Now he left them and walked over to the three American bodies. He stood looking down at them for a moment, then he raised his hand with the thumb extended, the forefinger and middle finger raised, and the ring finger and little finger folded. It was the traditional sign of the cross, preparatory to the bestowing of the blessing.

"No!" Gonzales shouted to the priest. "You will not bless these gringos."

"They are God's children," the priest replied. "I cannot, in good conscience, let any of God's children enter the hereafter without proper rites."

"Why bother? They are probably not even Catholic," Gonzales said.

"They are still God's children."

"They killed Juan Reyna. They are murderers. Let them go to hell."

"I cannot do that. I will bless them," the padre said.

Gonzales pulled his pistol and pointed it at the priest. When he pulled the hammer back, it made a deadly double-click as the sear engaged the cylinder. "If you bless them, I will kill you where you stand," he said in a cold flat voice.

Upon hearing the deadly words, the assembled villagers gasped in surprise.

The padre stared at Gonzales for a long moment. Gonzales continued to hold the gun on him, the barrel unwavering. The villagers were absolutely quiet. Then, resolutely making the sing of the cross, the priest made his blessing.

Gonzales's face grew almost purple-red and the vein in his temple began to throb. His eyes narrowed and his lips curled into a snarl.

"*Hijo de puta!*" he shouted, enraged by the priest's actions. Still, he put the pistol away, shoving it back into his holster.

Again the villagers gasped, this time over the audacity of their police chief calling a priest the son of a whore. Many of them prayed silently for the soul of Gonzales, who surely had damned himself by such a rash act. Others made the sign of the cross for the prayer that was answered, in that Gonzales did not kill the priest as he had threatened.

Ortega watched it all. Then he walked over and looked down at the bodies of Ken, Tennessee, and Chad. Even though he had ridden the trail with them, had camped out with them, shared food and canteen with them, he felt absolutely no sense of sorrow.

"So, Senor Tennessee," Ortega said quietly, "you are not so full of fight now, are you?" Ortega looked over toward Gonzales, who, after being showed up by the priest, was walking away, mumbling to himself.

"Sargento," Ortega called to him.

Gonzales stopped and turned toward Ortega. "Sí?"

Ortega waved his hand toward the bodies. "Who are these gringos? What happened here?"

Gonzales stared at Ortega for a moment. "Do I know you, senor?"

"No. I am from Mexico City," Ortega lied.

"I believe I have seen you."

"Impossible. I've never been here before," Ortega said. "These men, what happened?"

"They are very bad men," Gonzales said. "In Texas, they killed a father and son. Then they stole the wife and daughters. I believe they are going to sell the women to the *bandidos* in the hills."

"They made the mistake of coming to your village," Ortega suggested.

A large smile spread across Gonzales's face, and he nodded enthusiastically over the unexpected endorsement.

With his pride somewhat restored, Gonzales walked back toward the three American bodies. The priest was just finishing his blessing.

"They made a mistake," Gonzales said loudly, pointing to the three bodies. "They came to Escalon." He tapped his breast with the ends of his fingers. "They came to my village," he added. "And you can see what happens to outlaws who come to my village."

One of the black-shawled women who had been weeping over the bodies of the Mexicans now looked over toward Gonzales. She was surprised to see that the man who was standing behind Gonzales was the same man she had encountered at the well. That man had identified himself as the chief of the gringos. Could this possibly be the same person?

Her eyes were old and not as good as they once were, and she could not be sure until she got a closer look. So she started walking toward him.

Ortega saw the old woman almost as quickly as she saw him. He saw, too, that she was moving closer for a better look. That meant that she wasn't yet sure of his identity, but she had a strong suspicion. And as soon as she recognized him, she would make the connection between him and the three dead Americans.

Slowly but deliberately, Ortega remounted. With a small click of his tongue, he turned his horse away from the plaza.

"It is him," the old woman said. Raising a shaking hand, she pointed a long, bony finger toward Ortega. "He was with them."

No one paid any attention to her.

"He was with them," the old woman said again, loudly this time, and she got Gonzales's attention.

"What are you talking about old woman?" Gonzales said.

"'When the gringos came into the village, that man was riding with them," the old woman said. "I gave him water to drink. He told me he was their chief."

Ortega immediately slapped his feet against the sides of his horse. The animal bolted forward like a ball from a cannon.

"I knew I had seen him before!" Gonzales said. He turned toward Ortega just in time to see the horse bolt forwards. "*Alto!*" he shouted.

Ortega bent low over the horse's neck. Gonzales drew his pistol, and this time he didn't hesitate to use it. He fired, but missed.

"Shoot him!" Gonzales shouted. "Someone shoot him!"

Angrily, Gonzales looked around at the others. "Pull your weapons, you idiots! Shoot him! He is one of the murderers!"

Bullets now whistled by Ortega's head as he

pounded his heels into the animal's back. Not one bullet hit him.

"After him! After him! We must run him down!" Gonzales shouted.

Despite Gonzales's urgings, there was very little likelihood that Ortega could be run down. None of the villagers were mounted, nor were any of the horses even saddled. Ortega made good his escape, leaving Gonzales to fume in the dusty street, the sergeant's pistol still clutched tightly in his fist.

Because of his age, and because he was a natural leader listened to by the others, Jim Robison had become the undisputed ramrod of the little group of riders. Jim and his friends, along with Katie and her daughters, were camped for the night on the banks of a small, swiftly running stream. Here the water was cool and clear and they were able to fill their canteens and boil a pot of coffee. They cooked rice, augmented by a couple of rabbits, some wild onions and freshly picked mushrooms.

"What are we going to do if Ortega don't show up again?" Frank asked as they ate.

'We'll get the horses and start back without him," Jim said.

"How do you know they'll give 'em to us?"

"According to Clay Allison, the horses have already been bought and paid for. They have no choice in the matter. They'll have to give 'em to us," Jim insisted.

"Right. And if they don't, we'll just go to the law," Gene said. "That is, if the law don't shoot us as soon as they see us."

"We've got no problem with the law now," Barry said. "I mean, we've got the women with us. All we have to do is have them say it wasn't us that took 'em."

"And are they just going to forget about the men we killed back in Escalon?" Frank asked.

"So what do you think, Jim? What will we do about that?" Barry asked.

"Our best bet is just to get the horses, then get ourselves back on up to Texas," Jim answered. "I plan to shake the dirt of Mexico from my boots soon as I can."

"Texas, yes," Katie said. "That sounds good to me."

"I don't know why you are so anxious to get back," Marilou said. "There's nothing back there for us."

"What do you mean?" Katie asked.

"Pa's dead. Nate's dead. What's left?"

"The ranch," Katie said. "Your pa and I cleared land, battled Indians, drought, locusts, bankers, and Yankee carpetbaggers to build that ranch. There is no way I'm going to walk away from it now. We're going back to Texas to bury our dead. Then we'll get on with the livin'. It's what women have always done and we're no different."

As Jim listened to Katie talk to her daughters, he couldn't help but admire her. He had never taken himself a wife, had never really wanted to settle down. But now, seeing Katie with her daughters, he couldn't help but wonder if he hadn't missed out on something.

"We goin' to stay here for the night?" Frank asked.

"Yes," Jim said. "Frank, you take the first watch."

"Jim. Jim, you awake?"

Jim stirred in his bedroll, and Gene shook him again. "Wake up," he said.

Jim grunted.

"Damn, the older you get, the harder you are to wake up."

"I'm awake," Jim said.

"Maybe it's time you quit cowboyin'," Gene suggested.

Jim sat up and ran his hand across his face, then scratched his scalp as he yawned. "I told you, I'm awake," he said.

"It's four o'clock. It's your watch."

Jim stood up, walked over to one side and urinated, then came back to sit down on a rock near his bedroll while he pulled on his boots.

"Anything happen during the night?" he asked.

"Not a thing," Gene said, pulling his own boots off. "What time we goin' to get started today?"

"I figure round sunup," Jim replied.

"Damn. It'll take me that long to get back to sleep," Gene said.

Despite his protestations, Gene fell asleep within minutes, his snoring joining that of the others in camp. Jim took a walk around the perimeter of the camp. Satisfied that everything was as it should be, he found a rock and sat down.

It wasn't too long afterward that he heard the noise. Pulling his gun from his holster, he moved quietly to investigate. A minute later he located the sound's source and, when he saw what it was, stopped dead in his tracks.

There, in the bright spill of predawn moonlight was Katie Kincaid standing in the stream of water, totally nude. She was taking a bath, and because she had no soap, she was using the grit of a handful of sand. The result made her skin pink and shiny.

Jim caught his breath. He didn't like the idea of spying on the woman in her private moment, but he could barely take his eyes off her. He knew she was a handsome woman, but he had no idea how beautiful she really was.

Katie seemed intent on scrubbing her body, rubbing herself down with sand so hard that Jim thought she was about to rub herself raw. At first, he couldn't understand why she was so intense with her bath. Then he realized exactly what she was doing, and his heart went out to her.

Katie Kincaid was trying to wash away all the degradation and humiliation she had suffered over the last several days. And at that moment it dawned on Jim that, by spying on her, he might actually be adding to her humiliation, so he turned and started to walk away.

"You needn't leave, Mr. Robison," Katie said from the stream.

Jim was shocked by the words. He had no idea she even knew he was here. He stopped.

"I'm sorry. I didn't mean to intrude," he said.

Katie emerged from the water dripping wet. She started toward him, but he stood riveted to the spot, his eyes still averted.

"You aren't intruding," she said. "I heard you making out the watch last night. I knew when you would have the watch, so I chose this time to take my bath. You turn around, Mr. Robison," she said.

Jim turned, then gasped. He had seen naked women, of course, but they had all been whores, often wasted by dissipation. Katie Kincaid had lived a difficult life, but it was one made up of hard work and clean living. As a result, her body was firm and well-toned. Whereas the whores Jim had encountered often had large pillowy breasts, Katie's breasts were small and well formed, and he was keenly aware of her tightly drawn and sharply protruding nipples.

"I have to know," Katie said.

"I beg your pardon?"

"I have to know," Katie said again. "The men I was with: Shardeen, Whitey, and Red. They used me, degraded me. I have to know if any normal man will ever want me again."

"I promise you, Mrs. Kincaid," Jim said, "that's not something you need to worry about."

"Thank you,' Katie said. Without another word, she turned and walked away from him, disappearing into the morning darkness. Jim stood there for a long moment afterward, wondering if the encounter had really happened. Or if it was merely a hallucination, brought on by a trick of fatigue and shadow.

Chapter 14

When the sun came up, Clay Allison was sitting out on the hotel balcony, holding his hand to his aching jaw. The pain had kept him awake all night and he was now groggy and irritable.

He took a drink of whiskey, swirled it around in his mouth, then spat it out. He had been doing that throughout the night and, so far, had gone through three bottles. It seemed to help some, but it was a terrible waste of whiskey.

Clay had come into town the day before to have his aching tooth pulled. The dentist didn't believe in using chloroform, nor did he offer a tincture of laudanum. As a result, the extraction had been extremely painful. Clay accepted it, however, as being necessary for the greater good of getting rid of his toothache.

It now seemed, however, that it was all for naught. The pain of the extraction had eased, but the toothache was still there. Clay spent the night in agony, waiting until the dentist opened his office again so he could go see him.

Gradually, the little town began to come awake. A loaded freight wagon rolled slowly out of town. The smell of sizzling bacon began drifting up the street. Across from the hotel, the proprietor of the general store opened his doors, then stepped out onto the porch wearing a clean, white apron and began sweeping. Down the street the blacksmith started working, and the ringing of his hammer played counterpoint to the scratch of the broom.

Finally Clay saw a small, nearly bald man with rimless glasses walking up the sidewalk, heading toward the dental office. Dr. Chidister was whistling a jaunty little tune as he sauntered along. He reached his dental office, marked by the hanging sign of a tooth, opened the door, and went in. The little sign in the window was turned from CLOSED to OPEN.

"It's about damn time you came to work," Clay mumbled angrily.

Clay stood up from his chair, rinsed his

mouth out with whiskey one more time, spat over the balcony railing without regard as to who or what was below, then followed that with a healthy swallow. He had been going through the same procedure all night, rinsing, spitting, then drinking. As a result he was very drunk.

Clay left the hotel and walked across the street to the dentist's office. An old man with white hair and a beard was sitting in the dental chair. His head was tipped back and his mouth was open. Clay's entrance into the office wasn't a quiet one. He slammed the door hard behind him, causing both doctor and patient to look around.

"Get out," Clay said to the patient. He indicated the front door with a jerk of his hand.

"What?" the patient asked.

"See here, you can't come in here and run my patients off like that," the dentist said.

"Yeah, I can," Clay said easily. He pulled his pistol and cocked it, then looked directly at the patient. "Ain't that right, Mr. Peabody?"

"That's right, Mr. Allison," Peabody said, getting up from the chair and taking off the apron Dr. Chidister had draped around him. Peabody worked as a clerk in the leather goods store and knew Clay Allison by sight. In fact, as Clay's ranch was so close by, most knew him by sight. And all knew him by reputation.

Clay waited until Peabody was gone. Then he climbed into the dental chair.

"I must say, Mr. Allison, you do have a way of getting someone's attention. Now what can I do for you?"

"My tooth is still hurting," Clay said.

Chidister laughed lightly. "Oh, I'm afraid that is quite impossible."

"You may think it is impossible, but I'm telling you it's still hurting," Clay said. "Fact is, the son of a bitch is killing me. See what you can do about it."

"All right, let me have a look," Chidister said, leaning down over Clay's open mouth. He looked down inside, then clucked his tongue and shook his head. "Oh, my, this is awful. How could this have happened?"

"How could what happen?" Clay mumbled through his open mouth.

Chidister cleared his throat, nervously. "Mr. Allison, uh, we all make mistakes," he said.

"Mistakes? What kind of mistakes?"

"A rather big mistake, I'm afraid," Chidister said. "I'm going to have to pull the tooth that is bothering you."

"Wait a minute. Didn't you pull that tooth yesterday?"

"I'm afraid not. I, uh, pulled the wrong tooth," Chidister said.

"What!" Clay bellowed, yelling so loudly that people half a block away could hear him.

"I'm terribly sorry," Chidister said. "But such things happen all the time. I'm not the first person to make such a mistake."

"Well, you are the first person ever to make a mistake like that on me," Clay said. Although he had just put his gun away, he pulled it again and jammed the barrel into Chidister's belly. "Now you make sure to pull the right one this time."

"Y-y-y-yes, sir," Chidister stuttered.

Because he was frightened and nervous, Chidister's hands fumbled and quaked as he worked in Clay's mouth. Allison let out a bellow of pain as Chidister, dripping with sweat, finally pulled the tooth out, then held it up for Clay to see.

"Here it is," he said. "As you can see, it is rotten with decay." He smiled. "I reckon I got the right one this time."

"Why didn't you get it right the last time, you son of a bitch?"

"I'm sorry, Mr. Allison," the dentist said.

"Get in the chair," Allison ordered.

"I beg your pardon?"

"Are you deaf? I said get in the chair!"

"No, sir. Of course I'm not deaf. I just don't understand what you want," Chidister said as he sat down.

Clay picked up the pulling pliers, still dripping with his own blood and saliva. "Open your mouth," he ordered.

"What?" Chidister asked in a weak voice, beginning to understand what Clay had in mind.

"I said open your damn mouth," Clay said. "You owe me two teeth, and I aim to take 'em."

"Mr. Allison, you . . . you can't be serious!"

"Oh, I'm dead serious. Open your mouth, friend. I'm either going to pull two of your teeth, or I'm going to blow your brains out. And it makes me no never mind either way. What's it goin' to be, Doc? Do I kill you? Or do I pull a few of your teeth? It's up to you."

By that evening, there wasn't anyone in town who didn't know the story of Clay Allison pulling two of Dr. Chidister's teeth. Chidister was not a popular man in town. As a dentist, he was rough-handed, and the fact that he didn't use any painkillers—claiming that he didn't believe in them, though others said he was too cheap to use them—made his extractions even more painful.

As it turned out, Clay Allison wasn't the

first person to have the wrong tooth pulled. As a result, several people wanted to express their thanks to him for doing something they would like to have done but lacked the nerve to do so.

The good citizens of the town expressed their thanks by buying drinks. By nightfall, Clay had long forgotten about his toothache. He was so drunk that he no longer felt anything. His state of inebriation created a condition that he seldom experienced. He was unable to perform when he took Hazel Lee up to her room above the Silver Nugget Saloon.

"It's all right, honey," Hazel Lee said when, after an outburst of frustration, Clay Allison swung his legs over the edge of the bed and sat up. "It happens to lots of men."

"Well, it ain't never happened to me," Clay said.

"You're just tired, that's all. You didn't sleep none last night, what with your toothache and all. And you been goin' all day, besides. Why, it's only natural that you can't get it up right now."

"Ain't nothin' natural about it a'tall," Clay said. Getting up, he walked over to the window, and looked down on the street of the town. It was quite busy tonight as men moved from sa-

loon to saloon. "Look at 'em all down there,"
he said.

"Beg pardon, honey?" Hazel Lee said from
her bed.

Clay looked over toward her. She was not a
small woman, and as she lay on her back, her
large breasts looked like giant folds of flesh. She
was pockmarked and hairy. He had never had
any problems before with her, but perhaps he
had never really looked at her before, as he was
looking at her now.

"Damn," Clay said. "You are one ugly woman—
do you know that, Hazel Lee?"

"What?"

"How the hell is a man supposed to get it up
with someone like you?"

Hazel Lee sat up in bed, then pulled the bed
cover to shield herself against his cold glare.

"You, sir, are no gentleman," she said, mus-
tering as much dignity as she could under the
circumstances. "And I would appreciate it if you
would leave my room."

"Hell yes, I'll leave your room," Clay said,
resolutely. "The longer I look at you, the uglier
you get."

Clay put on his hat, then sat on a chair and
pulled on his boots. After that, he strapped on
his pistol. Except for the hat, boots, and pistol
belt, he was totally naked.

"I will go now," he said with a belch. "By your leave, madam."

Hazel Lee pointed to his shirt and pants and started to mention to him that he had forgotten something. Then, with a small smile, she let her hand drop.

"By your leave," Hazel Lee replied.

All conversation in the saloon stopped as Clay Allison tromped down the stairs. Everyone looked at him with horrified expressions on their faces, wanting desperately to laugh, but terrified to do so.

"What's the matter with everyone?" Clay asked. "Have I suddenly gone green?"

"No, Mr. Allison," the barkeep replied.

"Why are you all lookin' at me?"

Instantly, everyone looked away.

Clay pushed through the front door and stepped out onto the boardwalk outside. Two men were coming into the saloon at that moment, and they looked at Clay with their mouths open in shock.

"What are you looking at?" Clay demanded.

Without answering him, the men pushed through the batwing doors to go inside.

When Clay stepped into the middle of the street, he saw that several people were now looking at him, pointing and laughing. Angrily, Clay pulled his pistol.

"By God, the next son of a bitch who looks at me is goin' to get hisself shot!" Clay shouted. He began firing his gun, shooting holes through signs, shooting out the windows in Dr. Chidister's office, shooting holes in a couple of watering troughs so that the water began gurgling out into the street.

Not until he was out of bullets and looked down to his cartridge belt to punch out some more shells did he see that he wasn't wearing any clothes. Then, slowly, he turned and walked back into the saloon.

"I forgot my pants," he said, trying to make the words as nonchalant as if he had walked out of the saloon without his hat. He started up the stairs, got about halfway to the top, then felt an overpowering tiredness overtake him. "I'll just take a little nap," he said. Lying down right there halfway between the ground floor and the upper landing, Clay Allison passed out.

Chapter 15

Shardeen climbed up onto a rock from which he could see for nearly two miles back across the Sonoran Desert. A small rise hid everything beyond that point.

"See anything?" Whitey asked.

"No," Shardeen answered. Shardeen took the last swallow from a whiskey bottle, then tossed it against a nearby rock. The bottle shattered into several pieces.

"Dammit, Shardeen, what the hell did you go and break that bottle for?" Whitey complained. "We coulda sold that bottle for three or four centavos."

"Three or four centavos?" Shardeen snorted. "If I wanted to sell something that cheap, I'd sell that gold tooth of your'n."

"You ain't never goin' to get your hands on my tooth," Whitey said.

"It's prob'ly not even real gold," Shardeen answered. "But it don't matter none, 'cause once we get them womenfolk back, we'll sell 'em to the Mexican *bandidos*, just like we started out to."

"Yeah, well, we ain't got 'em yet," Whitey said.

"We'll get 'em. They can't get far, not on their own, anyhow."

"I don't know 'bout that. They've done pretty good on their own so far. They got away from us and they spooked our horses so that it took us half a day to get 'em back. Besides which, they also kilt Red."

"Red getting kilt ain't no big loss, believe me," Shardeen said. "If they hadn't kilt him, I most likely would done it myself. That boy was just too damn stupid to live."

"Hey, Shardeen, lookie there," Whitey said, pointing off in the distance. "I think they're a-comin'."

"No, it couldn't be," Shardeen said. "There's too many of 'em."

Whitey shielded his eyes with his hand and squinted off into the distance.

"The hell it ain't them," Whitey said. "Take a good look."

Studying the distant party of riders, Shardeen saw that it was, indeed, the three women who had made good their escape. He saw, too, that they weren't alone, for they were in the company of four men.

"What the hell?" Shardeen said aloud.

"Who do you reckon them men are?" Whitey asked.

"Like as not, someone who's wantin' to do what we was goin' to do," Shardeen said.

"What? You mean someone who's plannin' to sell the women?"

"Yes," Shardeen said. "*Our* women."

Whitey studied the approaching riders for a moment longer. "I don't know," he said. "You ask me, them women don't look captured. Looks to me like they're ridin' with 'em by choice."

Shardeen spit out a stream of tobacco juice. "Yeah, well, it don't matter none whether they stole 'em or the women went to 'em. All that matters is, they got the women and we don't."

"Sons of bitches," Whitey said. "And they's four of them to only two of us."

"Yeah, well, get your rifle," Shardeen ordered. "We'll take 'em out 'fore they even know we're here."

"Two of us against four of them? That don't make too much sense if you ask me."

"Just don't miss with your first shot," Shardeen said as he moved into position with his rifle.

Jim heard the angry buzz of a bullet sizzling past his ear even before he heard the sound of the shot. He knew instantly what it was, and he shouted at the others as he spurred his horse to get off the trail.

"What's up?" Barry asked.

"Someone's shootin' at us!"

The other men reacted instantly to the warning, for they were trail-wary and knew the danger of hesitation. But the women were less responsive and they paused for a moment, unsure of what was going on or what to do. They were spared only because Shardeen didn't want them hit. The women would be worthless to him dead.

When a second bullet kicked up dirt nearby, then whined on beyond them, Katie jumped into action. "Follow the men!" she shouted, kicking her own horse. Her two daughters followed suit.

A short, quick gallop brought them to a ridgeline that was extended by an outcropping of rocks. All seven of them dashed behind the cover, putting the ridge between them and the shooters.

Jim swung down from his horse, his rifle in hand. Frank, Barry, and Gene joined him. The girls dismounted and also sought safety behind the rocks. Katie grabbed the reins of all seven horses.

"What are you doing? Get down!" Jim shouted when he saw her.

"You want these horses to bolt?" Katie asked. "I have no intention of being left afoot."

With a nod of assent, Jim waved her on up the ridgeline, even as bullets were whistling overhead. Jim crawled up to the top of the ridge and looked across the draw to the rocks on the other side. As he was looking, he saw two flashes as their assailants snapped off another couple of shots at them.

"Shoot at them!" Jim shouted. "Keep their heads down!"

Frank, Barry, and Gene began firing, jacking shells into their rifle chambers, firing, then working the lever again. In this way they kept up a deadly fusillade that kept their assailants at bay. That was exactly what Jim wanted, for it gave him the opportunity to slip, unobserved, to a location about twenty-five yards down the ridge. When he was in position he gave the signal for the other three to stop shooting.

Abrubtly, the gunfire stopped, chased by returning echoes from across the ridge. There was a long period of silence and Jim held his finger to his lips, indicating to Barry and the others that he wanted the cease-fire maintained.

"What happened to 'em?" Jim heard a voice ask. It was the voice of one of the assailants.

"I don't know," another voice answered.

"You think they skedaddled?"

"Stick your head up there and have a look."

That was what Jim was waiting for. Laying his cheek alongside the walnut stock of his Winchester, he peered through the rear sight, centered the front sight, and waited.

He almost pulled the trigger when he saw a hat come up, but he held his fire. He was glad he did when he realized that the hat was on the end of a rifle.

A moment after the hat disappeared behind the rock, it reappeared, this time on someone's head. Jim squeezed the trigger.

The rifle boomed and kicked back against his shoulder. Through the drifting smoke of the discharge, Jim saw the assailant slump forward, his rifle clattering down the rocks in front of him, finally ending up on the ground below.

"Whitey?" a voice called. "Whitey, you hit?"

Jim jacked another shell into the chamber and waited for another head to appear, but there was none. Instead, he heard the clatter of hoof-beats as a horse galloped away.

"They're runnin'!" Frank called. He started to climb up for a better look, but Jim held out a cautioning hand.

"Wait," Jim said. "That was only one horse."

"You think they's more of 'em?" Barry asked.

"I don't know. Hard to figure only two men attacking four."

"Maybe not," Frank said. "Bein' as they were in good position like that, could be they figured on droppin' two of us with the first two shots. Then the odds would be even and they would still have the position."

"That's true," Jim agreed. He rubbed his cheek for a moment. "All right, I'll have a look."

Warily, Jim climbed over the top of the ridgeline he had been using for cover. Then he started across an opening toward the next ridge. He kept his eyes on the crest, waiting for any shape or shadow that might show up against the skyline. But nothing appeared.

Paying no immediate attention to the body, Jim climbed to the top of the ridge from which the assailants had staged their ambush. He looked around. Except for one rider in the distance, he saw no one. Climbing back up to the crest, he waved his hand over his head, signaling that all was clear.

Frank, Barry, and Gene jogged across the opening then. They were followed a moment later by Katie and her daughters. The women had divided up the horses so that she was leading three, while each of her daughters led two.

Jim was looking down at the body when the others arrived. The blood around the bullet hole in the slain man's temple seemed exceptionally crimson when contrasted with the man's white hair and nearly white skin.

"Damn," Gene said. "Look at that. I don't think I ever seen a body get so pale so fast."

"He always looked like that," Kate said, arriving at that moment. "They called him Whitey."

Jim recalled then that he had heard someone shout that name out during the fight.

"What would make a fella so pasty-faced?" Gene asked.

"I don't know," Katie admitted.

"He's what they call an albino," Jim explained.

"An albino? I'll be damned. I've heard of them. Don't think I've ever seen one before," Gene said.

Jim looked at Katie. "Is this one of the men who captured you?" he asked.

"Yes," Katie replied. "The son of a bitch who got away is called Shardeen."

"Mama!" Brenda gasped. "I thought you told us never to use words like that."

"I did," Katie replied. "But I also told you to always tell the truth. And the only way you can refer to Shardeen truthfully is to call him a son of a bitch."

Jim and the others laughed at Katie's declaration, yet they were all respectfully aware of the reason she spoke of him in such vitriolic terms.

Shardeen rode hard, looking over his shoulder often to see if anyone was following him. It hadn't been a very smart move, firing on four men like that. But he figured if he and Whitey could get one apiece with the opening shots, they could kill the other two before they even realized what was happening to them. Then the women would've been easy pickings. It would've worked, too, if that damn Whitey hadn't missed.

Hell, it was all Whitey's fault. As far as Shardeen was concerned, gettin' hisself killed was good enough for the son of a bitch.

Shardeen had had enough of Mexico with its rocks, desert, cacti, scorpions, and Mexicans. He didn't care if he never heard another word of Spanish, and he didn't care if he never saw those damned women again.

Chapter 16

Hector Ortega was having a drink when someone came into the cantina with news that seven gringos had just ridden into the village of Durango. The number was significant to Ortega, because he had left Texas with seven gringos. But three had been killed back in Escalon. So how could there still be seven?

"How many gringos did you say there were?" Ortega asked.

"Seven. Four men and three women."

Four men, Ortega thought. That number was right. If three of them had been killed at Escalon, then there would be four remaining. But who were the women? Where had they come from?

Ortega recalled, then, that he had heard something about a group of Americans capturing three women, a mother and two daughters. And even though he knew that Jim Robison and the others weren't guilty of that, the village of Escalon had thought them to be, thus bringing on the gunfight.

Ortega poured a glass of tequila for the man who had brought the information. "Senor, the three women. Tell me about them."

The man with the information held up his glass. "Gracias," he said. Before answering, he drank his drink; then he wiped his mouth with the back of his hand. "What do you wish to know?"

"Is one old and the others young?"

The man with the information grabbed his crotch. "The old one is not too old, and the young ones are not too young," he said with a leering grin.

The others laughed.

"It is the mother and daughters," Ortega said, almost to himself. "How is it that they are with my *vaqueros*?"

"Your *vaqueros*, senor? But they are gringos. How can they be your *vaqueros*?"

"Gringos, yes," Ortega said. "But they are my *vaqueros*, because I am their chief," he said with haughty bluster. "Perhaps I had better go see these men and learn why they have three women with them."

* * *

Jim and the men were watering the horses while Katie and her daughters had gone into a store to buy some much needed supplies. Barry was the one who first saw Ortega coming toward them, picking his way gingerly through the horse droppings in the plaza.

"Well, now, lookie here," Barry said. "If it isn't our long-lost pard."

"That son of a bitch ain't no pard of mine," Frank insisted.

"Mine, either," Gene said.

"Take it easy, boys," Jim said. "He has to be our pard for a little while longer. At least until we get the horses back to Clay Allison."

"All right, if you say so, Jim. I reckon I'll go along with it for now," Frank said. "But once we get them horses delivered, me and the senor there, is goin' to have us a little set-to."

Ortega pasted a big smile on his face as he approached the men. "I have been waiting for you," he said. "Where have you been? We have work to do."

"Where have *we* been?" Jim replied. "We waited in Escalon for you, just as you said. Why didn't you come back?"

"Oh, I did come back," Ortega said. "But when I returned, I learned that there had been a big fight between you and the poor people of the village. You are not very popular in my country now, senors. I am told that you killed many of my people."

"As far as I'm concerned, we didn't kill enough of them," Frank said. "They started shootin' at us for no reason."

"They believed they had a reason," Ortega said. "They believed you to be the men who captured three white women." Looking up, he saw Katie, Marilou, and Brenda coming back from the store, carrying several packages. "These women, perhaps?" he added. He smiled again, bowed slightly, and touched the brim of his sombrero. "*Buenas días*, senora and senoritas."

"Who is this?" Katie asked.

"This is Hector Ortega," Jim said. "He is the hombre I told you about, the fella who knows where the horses are." Jim looked pointedly, at Ortega. "You do know where the horses are, don't you?"

"Sí, senor," Ortega answered.

"Well, if you don't mind, lead us to them and let's get started back. I don't mean no offense to your country and all, but I do believe I've had just about as much of Mexico as I can stomach."

"You got that right," Gene said.

"Yeah, I'd like to get started back today," Frank added.

Ortega shook his head. "I don't think you can

get started back today. I think, maybe, it will take one week."

"One week? Why so long?" Jim asked.

"The horses," Ortega said. "Senor Allison will want the horses broken before we take them to him, I think."

"The horses aren't broken? You mean you've brought us all the way down here to round up a bunch of wild horses?" Jim asked, angrily.

"You will not have to gather the horses," Ortega said. "The horses have already been caught and are in a corral. But Senor Allison wants them broken before we deliver them."

"Nobody said anything about breaking horses," Gene said.

"I think maybe if you knew you would not come," Ortega replied.

"You're damn right we wouldn't have come," Gene added.

"Look here, Oretega. Are you telling us that Allison knew about this? And he expects us to break five hundred horses?" Barry asked.

"Sí, this is true, I think."

"What do you think, Jim?" Frank asked.

"I don't know," Jim replied. "Before we lost Tennessee, Chad, and Ken, maybe we could've done it. But being as we're three men short, I just don't know."

"I know some men," Ortega said. "They will

work for not very much money. They will help break the horses."

"So what are we going to do, Jim?"

Jim sighed and stroked his chin. "I don't see that we have much choice in the matter," he said. "We've been through a lot to get here. Damn if I'm going to go back home without them horses." He looked at Ortega. "Where are they?"

"They are very near," Ortega answered.

"All right, take us to them. Then get me three, no, make it five men who are good with horses."

"Sí, senor."

Frank laughed loudly at the sight of Barry rolling in the dirt after having been thrown. "That was about the funniest thing I ever seen," he said, still chuckling.

"Maybe you ought to try and ride that one, Frank," Gene suggested.

"If I do, you can bet I'll do a lot better job than Barry just did."

"How much better?"

"I'll stay on him."

"Think so?" Gene asked.

"Five dollars says I will. Bring him over here," Frank said. "I'll ride him without bein' throwed even once."

"That's a pretty high order you've set for yourself," Gene said.

"Ain't settin' it no higher'n I can do," Frank insisted. "You won't see me rollin' in the dirt like our friend here." He nodded toward Barry, who was using the crown of his Stetson to brush off the seat of his pants.

"Maybe I'll just take you up on that little bet," Gene said.

The place where the boys were working the horses was about five miles south of Durango. They had set up camp there, and for two days they and the five Mexican riders Ortega found had been breaking horses.

Begrudgingly, Jim had to admit that the Mexican riders were quite good because they were halfway through breaking the entire herd. Much further along than he would have ever believed possible.

Katie and her two daughters had set up their own camp right alongside the boys, making themselves useful by cooking the meals and by separating the horses that were broken and those that weren't.

Barry looked at Frank, contemplating the wager Gene had just made with him.

"All right, Mr. Smarty Pants, if you are serious about that five-dollar bet you just made with Gene, how 'bout lettin' me have some of it?"

"You got it. Ricardo!" Frank called to one of the squat, serious-looking *vaqueros* they had hired. "Bring that cayuse over here!"

With the promise of a little entertainment, the others quit what they were doing and climbed the fence to sit on the top rail so that they could watch. Even Jim was interested in seeing whether or not Frank could make good on his wager. Katie and her two daughters came over to watch as well. They stood on the ground and looked through the rails.

The horse, jerking against the lead and kicking up its back feet, showed its protest at being in harness.

"Bring him over here to the fence," Frank said. "I need to get a good seat if I'm goin' to do this."

"You'll need more than a good seat," Gene said. "You'll need a miracle."

"Well, for five dollars I reckon I'll just call one of them up for you," Frank said, smiling. When the horse was in place, Frank climbed the fence, then swung his leg over the saddle, holding it there for a minute before he actually swung aboard.

"Well, what are you waiting for?" Gene teased him.

"Don't rush me," Frank replied. "To do somethin' like this you got to get it just right the first time."

There was an extended period of silence as everyone waited to see what would happen next. Slowly, the reins were passed up to Frank, while two men continued to hold the horse by its halter.

"Now!" Frank shouted.

The two men let go of the halter, and the horse exploded away from the fence. It jumped straight up, then came down on stiff legs before kicking up its hind quarters.

"Hang on, Frank! Hang on!" Barry called.

Then Frank did a strange thing. He leaned forward and took the horse's ear between his teeth. He chomped down.

The horse let out a whinny of pain.

When the horse bucked harder, Frank bit harder. When the horse eased up, Frank eased up. It didn't take the horse long to learn the lesson. The more it bucked, the more severe the pain in his ear. The less he bucked, the less severe. After a matter of only a few seconds, the bucking stopped altogether.

"Hey! That ain't no fair!" Gene called. "You didn't say nothin' 'bout biting!"

"Yeah, but you didn't say he *couldn't* bite the horse's ear, either," Jim said, still laughing. "Looks like he beat you pretty good."

Frank, with a big smile on his face, and with the horse stepping out smartly and well under control, paraded the animal around the corral. The other men laughed and offered their congratulations.

"All right, here's your money," Gene said when Frank got down from the now broken horse.

"You are a gracious loser, my friend," Frank said as he relieved Gene of the money.

Chapter 17

Clay Allison was sitting in the back of the Silver Nugget Saloon in Alamosa, Colorado, drinking whiskey straight from the bottle and playing a game of solitaire. It had been several days since he had pulled the dentist's teeth, shot up the town wearing only his hat, then passed out naked on the saloon stairs.

Since that time men, women, and even the children pointed him out on the street, laughing as they told and retold the story of him lying "shiny-ass-up on the stairs."

It was an unfamiliar situation for Clay. He was used to being feared, not ridiculed. In addition, Clay was normally a gregarious man who depended upon social intercourse, friendly games of chance, and a certain degree of hero worship. Now that he was the target of derision, few people wanted anything to do with him. As a result, he started withdrawing more and more into himself, drinking more and more as he did so.

Outside the saloon at that moment, Will Shardeen had just ridden into town. The outlaw dismounted, then tied his horse off at the hitching rack in front of the saloon. Tired, filthy, and dispirited, he showed the results of several days of hard riding.

As Shardeeen stepped up onto the wooden porch in front of the saloon, he pulled a handful of change from his pocket. In the palm of his dirty hand, he counted forty-three cents. Barely the price of two drinks. It was fairly obvious that he was going to have to do something to get some more money, and he was going to have to do it very soon.

The saloon wasn't terribly busy inside. Two men, both teamsters, were standing at the bar. As they drank their beer, they engaged each other in an argument about the relative merits of mules versus draft horses. A card game was in progress at one table, while at another, a cowboy with no money tried to talk a soiled dove into taking him on credit. In the back of the room, Shardeen saw one man alone playing a game of solitaire. From the jerky awkwardness of his movements as he manipulated the cards, it was easy to see that he was drunk.

Shardeen never entered any saloon without a careful appraisal of everyone present. He knew that there was paper out on him. In addition, he had made many enemies during his lifetime and he was well aware that at any bar, anywhere, one of these enemies might be waiting to strike.

Deciding that the saloon was safe, he slapped a coin down on the bar. "Whiskey," he said in a low, guttural grunt.

Smiling a greeting at his new customer, the barkeep poured a glass, then brought it down to Shardeen. As he approached, the smile left his face, and he turned up his nose in disgust at encountering Shardeen's fetid odor. Years of tending bar, however, had prepared him for such unpleasantness, and without uttering a disparaging word, he picked up the coin.

"Who's the drunk in the back of the room?" Shardeen asked.

The thought had crossed Shardeen's mind that the drunk might be someone he could lure out into the alley and relieve of any money he might be carrying.

"That there is Clay Allison," the barkeep replied, as he recorked the bottle.

Shardeen reacted in surprise, and he looked again at the lone card player.

"Clay Allison? Are you sure?"

"I've known him for a long time," the barkeep said. "That's Clay Allison."

Shardeen lifted the glass to his lips. "I didn't know he was a drunk."

"He don't stay drunk all the time," the barkeep replied. "But when he does get drunk, he is something to behold." The bartender laughed. "Not long ago, the dentist pulled the wrong tooth, so Allison got even with him by pulling a few of the dentist's teeth in return."

Shardeen laughed. "He pulled the dentist's teeth? That's a good one, all right."

"Yes, sir, folks round here got themselves a good laugh out of it. Only it ain't worked out all that good for Allison. Turns out the dentist is suin' Allison for ten thousand dollars. And most folks is thinkin' that Doc Chidister is goin' to get the money he's goin' after, seein' as there's no doubt that Allison really did pull them teeth."

"You say the dentist is suin' Allison for ten thousand dollars? Has Allison got that kind of money?"

"He's got that and a lot more besides," the barkeep answered.

"I thought he was nothin' more than a gun-fighter. How'd he come by money like that?"

"Ranchin', I suppose," the barkeep replied. "I hear tell he's got him a herd of horses comin' up from Mexico way. Five hundred head, they're sayin', and he aims to sell that herd to the army for fifty dollars a head."

"Fifty dollars a head? I ain't none too good at cipherin'," Shardeen said. "How much money would that be?"

"Twenty-five thousand dollars," the barkeep answered.

Shardeen had never seen anything close to that much money. He wasn't sure he could even imagine how much that was.

He turned his back to the bar and looked again at Allison, studying him over the rim of his glass. So this was the famous gunman? Well, the famous gunfighter didn't look like so much now.

After a gunfight, when Shardeen was the only one standing, he was sometimes compared to Clay Allison. Some said he was *nearly* as fast as Allison, some said he *was* as fast. Others had hinted that he was even faster.

For a long time now, Shardeen had wondered how he would stack up against the legend. He had always wanted to try the famous gunman, and he began thinking about it, contemplating a scenario in which he would come face-to-face with him while Allison was in his present condition. It would be an easy way to gain a reputation as the man who shot Clay Allison.

On the other hand, if he did that, he might be killing the goose that laid the golden eggs. If Clay Allison was about to get twenty-five thousand dollars, Shardeen planned on finding some way to get his hands on all that money. He turned back to the bar with a small smile on his face. Maybe things were beginning to look up after all. Ordering another drink, Shardeen began thinking about what he would do with twenty-five thousand dollars.

Even as he was thinking of the grand prize, he began to wonder how he was going to survive the next few days. He was going to have to find some money, somewhere, soon.

At that moment, a young cowboy came into the saloon and stood just inside the door for a few seconds, looking around the room. Finally he saw what he was looking for. Clay Allison.

"Mr. Allison," the cowboy called, starting toward him.

"Who's the ranny?" Shardeen asked.

"That's Billy Proxmire," the barkeep replied. "He's one of Allison's cowboys."

"What do you want, Billy?" Allison asked, not bothering to look up from his game of solitaire.

"Mr. Allison, I expect you better come back out to the ranch," Billy said. "There's likely to be some trouble."

Allison stared hard at the young cowboy, trying to focus, though the fact that he had been drunk for the last twenty-four hours made any kind of concentration difficult. His eyes appeared to swim in their sockets.

"What kind of trouble?"

"Your brother-in-law is here."

"Jason Wilson? What's that no-account son of a bitch want?"

Billy cleared his throat. It was obvious that he was about to tell his boss something that Allison wasn't going to want to hear.

"Uh, Mr. Wilson says you are embarrassin' the entire family by all your drinkin' and carryin' on, and he plans to put a stop to it."

"Oh, he did, did he? And did he tell you just how he plans to do that?"

Billy cleared his throat again. "Uh, yes, sir. He said he was going to beat some sense into you."

"Well, now, we'll just see who is going to beat some sense into who," Clay said, standing so quickly that he tipped his chair over. Angrily, he started toward the front door, but he was so drunk that he reeled as he went, falling into one table, lurching into another. "Get out of my way!" he shouted.

"Mr. Allison, you want to take my horse?" Billy called after him.

"Don't need it," Clay answered. "I drove the buckboard in."

"Yes, sir, I know you did. But I'd feel better if you'd take my horse back to the ranch. Or better yet, why don't you let me drive you back?"

Clay stopped at the front door and looked back toward Billy. A mocking snarl caused Clay's lips to curl. "What are you trying to say, boy? That I can't drive a buckboard?"

"No, sir, I'm not saying that. I mean, I know you can," Billy replied. "But you have had a few drinks and it might be easier on you if you would let me drive."

Clay belched. "The day I let a little pissant like you drive me around is the day I'll hang up my spurs for good."

Shardeen had followed the entire exchange between Clay and Billy with interest. As the rancher and his anxious employee left the saloon, Shardeen moved to the front door to be able to follow them from there.

Shardeen had parked the buckboard in the

wagon yard across the street and about halfway down the block. He was so drunk that he could barely walk, lurching down the street as he made his way toward the wagon yard, staggering from side to side.

For a brief moment, Shardeen considered stepping out into the street and calling him out. He could kill Allison easily, and no one could accuse him of not facing the other man fair and square in the street. But as much as he wanted the reputation such an act would give him, he wanted the money more.

When Clay Allison reached his buckboard, he stopped for a minute and began retching. After a few dry heaves, he threw up by the back wheel of the buckboard. Then, wiping his mouth with his sleeve, he untied the team and climbed in.

To Shardeen's surprise, Clay didn't sit down. Instead he stood just in front of the seat and steered the team out of the yard. Once they were clear of the yard, he picked up a whip and snapped it over their heads, urging them into a gallop.

"No, Mr. Allison, sit down!" Billy called.

Clay shot a glance toward Billy. "I don't intend to let that no-account brother-in-law get away from me," Clay shouted as the team galloped by, the buckboard swaying and bouncing behind the team.

At the intersection of Main and Front, a boardwalk had been laid across the street to enable men and women to cross without soiling their trouser cuffs or skirt hems. The team leaped over the boards, but the front wheels of the buckboard hit it at an angle. Suddenly the wagon lurched violently, and Clay Allison was tossed off.

"Mr. Allison!" Billy shouted in warning, running toward him.

Clay flew through the air, flailing wildly with his hands. He hit the ground head-first.

Shardeen watched as Billy ran toward his boss, but Clay Allison's motionless form lay in a grotesquely twisted position in the muck and the mire of Front Street. It was obvious to everyone that he had broken his neck. Clay Allison, a man who had faced many a gunman in desperate fights, lay crumpled in the street, dead from a simple accident.

Shardeen just smiled.

Chapter 18

The boys were in pretty high spirits. They were two weeks on the trail, heading back home. The horses, though only recently broken, were well under control. Jim was riding point, Gene had the left flank, Barry the right, while Frank brought up the rear.

The women were helping as well, Jim having positioned them so that their mere presence would help keep the herd moving in the right direction. To do this, he put Brenda on the left and Marilou on the right. Katie was riding with him, and it was she who made the observation that her two daughters had changed places with each other, Marilou switching to the left while Brenda shifted to the right.

"Why did they do that?" Jim asked. "They didn't like where I put them?"

"It's not that they didn't like *where* you put them—it's that they had their own preference as to *who* you put them with," Katie replied. "Marilou prefers Gene, while Brenda is partial to Barry."

Jim chuckled. "I didn't know that."

"Well, you've been so busy getting the horses ready to drive back home that you haven't been paying any attention to the budding romances."

"Oh, wait a minute. This isn't good. If your daughters start pairing off with Gene and Barry, where does that leave Frank?"

"Sorry I don't have a third daughter," Katie said. "But I guess Frank will just have to be on his own."

"Yeah, I suppose so," Jim answered. "But he's a mite older than the other two. If he and I sort of get left out of this, I reckon we'll do all right."

"What makes you think you are being left out?" Katie asked.

"What do you mean?"

"Oh, for heaven's sake, Jim. Are you completely blind to what's going on around you? Do you think your seeing me bathing that day was an accident?"

Jim paused for a moment before he answered. "I wasn't sure it actually happened," he finally said.

"What?"

"I thought maybe I dreamed it," Jim explained.

Katie laughed out loud. "Well, tell me this, Mr. Jim Robison. Did you think it was a pleasant dream? Or was it a nightmare?"

"Oh, it was the best dream I ever had," Jim replied. "Better than the best dream, since now I know it wasn't a dream at all, that I really did see you nak—that is, I mean uh . . ." He paused, blushing in embarrassment.

Katie laughed again and put her hand on Jim's arm. "Maybe you'll have that dream again sometime soon," she suggested.

Katie's suggestive remarks, though welcomed by Jim, did make him uneasy, and he looked around quickly to make certain there was no one to overhear them.

"What are you looking around for? Are you afraid someone might have ridden up here just to listen to what we were talking about?"

"No, I, uh, was just wondering when Ortega would be getting back with our fresh supplies," Jim lied.

Ortega wasn't coming back with supplies. He was in Chihuahua at that very moment, meeting with Capitán Eduardo Bustamante.

"You say you know where the men who com-

mitted the murders in Escalon are," Bustamante said.

"Sí," Ortega said. "There is a reward for
them, is there not?"

"A very large reward," Bustamante answered.
"But I am sure, Senor, that you are not provid-
ing the information only for the reward. You are
doing it for the love of justice, are you not?"

"Sí," Ortega replied. "I am doing it for the
love of justice and my country."

And the fact that, with the others dead, the
herd of horses would be his, Ortega thought,
though he dared not say the words aloud.

"What do you think happened to Ortega?"
Frank asked as they were ready to break camp
the next morning.

"I don't know," Jim replied. "He should've
been back two or three days ago."

"Maybe the law got him," Gene suggested.

"Why would the law get Ortega?" Katie
asked.

"When we were coming down here, we found
a dodger on him," Jim said. "He claimed it was
for someone else who was also named Hector
Ortega. He said that was a very common name
in these parts."

"But none of us believed him," Barry said.

"Yeah, we all figured it was him," Gene added.

"Jim, we're going to need to know one way or the other if the law got him," Frank said. " 'Cause if he's been caught, then we're goin' to have to get our own supplies. As it is, we don't have enough to even make it back to the border, let alone all the way up to Colorado."

"I know," Jim said.

"If you'd like, I could ride on ahead, see what I can find out," Frank suggested. "And if I can't find him, I'll buy the supplies myself."

Jim stroked his chin. "I don't know, Frank. That could be a little risky," he said. "I'm not that keen on the idea of one of us separatin' from the others."

"Frank's right about one thing. We're going to have to have more supplies soon," Katie said. "We are almost out of everything."

"It may be risky," Frank said. "But I figure I'm as good a choice to take the chance as anyone. You might not have noticed, but our other two pards here have sorta fell in love. And I reckon you're a mite interested in Miz Katie yourself. That leaves me as the only one unattached, so to speak."

"Frank, listen. We didn't plan on nothin' like this," Gene started.

But Frank chuckled, and held up his hand to interrupt him. "Don't you boys be worryin' none about me," he said. "I'm fine with the idea. Truth to tell, I'm not ready to settle down with any one woman yet. I kinda like the sportin' girls that you find in the saloons. Uh, no offense meant to you and your daughters, Miz Katie."

Katie laughed. "No offense taken, Frank."

"So what about it, Jim? Shall I go on ahead this morning and see what I can find out about Ortega? Or do you want me to just forget about Ortega and get some supplies?"

Jim sighed. "One of us should go on ahead and find out what's going on," he said. "But I think I'm the one who should go."

"Why you and not me?" Frank asked.

"Because like it or not, I've taken on the role of leadin' this band of ragtag cowboys," Jim answered. "And I wouldn't be much of a leader if I sent someone else out to do what I should do myself."

"Jim, you're the leader, that's true," Katie said. "So don't you think your job should be here, with us?"

Jim shook his head. "No, I don't," he answered. "And you don't, either. You just want me here because you're worryin' about me."

"Perhaps I am worrying about you. Is that so bad?" Katie asked.

Jim smiled. "No, ma'am. I don't reckon there's anything at all bad about that. I sorta like someone worryin' about me. But this is somethin' I've got to do."

"But why . . . ?" Katie started.

"Don't try to stop him, Miz Katie," Frank said. "I'd rather go myself, but I know what Jim is talking about. If he stayed back now and let me go, he'd never feel right about it--especially if anything happened to me."

"Frank understands," Jim said. "I hope you do, too."

Katie nodded silently. Then she said, "Please promise me to be careful."

"Don't you worry about that," Jim said. "I intend to be extra careful. I like the way things are turnin' out between us."

It was late afternoon and Jim was several miles ahead of the trail outfit when the shot sounded. The crack of the rifle and the deadly whine of lead searing the air reached Jim's ears simultaneously. Only luck saved him. He had hunched forward in the saddle for a moment to adjust his rump just as the shot was fired. The bullet whizzed right by where his head had been an instant before.

Jim saw a puff of white smoke hanging in the air two hundred yards away. Flattening against his horse, he kicked it into a gallop and rode in a zigzag pattern toward the knoll below the little cloud of smoke. He drew his pistol and pointed it at the drifting white puff. If so much as a hair showed above the crest, he would blast it. He covered the two hundred yards in about fifteen seconds, charged around the knoll, then jumped from the saddle and rolled on the ground toward the cover of a nearby rock.

There was no one there.

Jim lay behind the rock for a long moment until he was absolutely sure he was alone. Then he moved cautiously over to where his attacker had waited in ambush. On the ground was the spent cartridge of a .44-40 jacked out of a Winchester by the assailant after firing. There were horse tracks nearby, and when Jim examined them, he was shocked to recognize the bar-tie shoe tracks of Ortega's horse.

The man who had shot at him was Ortega! But why?

"Well, Senor Ortega, I don't know what kind of a burr you got in your saddle," Jim said aloud, "but I reckon I'm just the man to take it out."

Jim swung back onto his horse and began following Ortega's tracks. The Mexican knew he was being tracked, and he did everything he could to throw Jim off. He rode across solid rock; he tied brush to his horse's tail to drag out tracks; he cut and recut his own trail. But, grim-faced, and determined, Jim hung on doggedly.

As he trailed Ortega, he wondered why Ortega had turned on them. Two possibilities came to mind. One was that, now that the horses were broken, Ortega might want to take over the herd for himself. The other possibility was that Ortega wanted the women, not for himself, but to sell to the *bandidos*. He knew that such an option wouldn't be unthinkable for a man like Ortega.

Jim trailed Ortega for the rest of the afternoon, until darkness fell. That night, he saw a campfire on the trail ahead of him. He was pretty sure it was a false campfire, set by the Mexican in hope of luring Jim into the camp. So Jim moved cautiously through the night until he reached Ortega's fire. Looking around carefully, he saw that he had been right. Ortega hadn't camped at that spot and had no intention of camping there.

Jim continued until he came to a range of steep, rocky hills. He was certain Ortega wouldn't try to navigate through there in the dark, and even if he did, Jim wouldn't be able to follow his tracks. He decided that there was nothing he could do but stop and wait for the light of day.

*   *   *

From the position of the stars, Jim supposed that it was about two o'clock in the morning. He had been sleeping lightly when something woke him up. He lay quietly for a few minutes, listening to the sounds in the night. Wind sighed through the dry limbs of a nearby mesquite tree, his horse whickered, but everything else was silent. Still, Jim sensed something amiss.

Quietly, Jim rolled up his poncho, then stuck it under his blanket. That done, he crawled over to a small depression, slipped down into it, and looked back at his bedroll. From his position, it looked like someone was still in the blankets.

There was a sudden flash of flame from a muzzle blast and the crack of a rifle shot. A puff of dust flew up from the bedroll. Jim knew that if he hadn't moved, he would be dead now.

Jim waited and listened. Finally, he heard what he was listening for. Someone was walking toward the camp, moving very quietly. Jim knew then that whoever it was, the would-be killer was coming in to finish him off at close range.

He waited for the nocturnal assassin to take his second shot. When he did fire again, Jim used the flame from the muzzle blast as a target. Aiming at the upper right-hand corner of the flame pattern, Jim pulled the trigger.

He heard a grunt of pain, then the sound of someone falling. Jim waited in the darkness.

"Senor Robison," the assailant called. The voice was racked with pain, but Jim recognized it as Ortega's. "Senor Robison, you have killed me, I think."

"Why did you try to kill me, Ortega?" Jim asked. Playing it safe, he still did not show himself.

"I thought it would be easier with you dead," Ortega said.

"Easier to do what?"

"To kill the others and take your women and your herd. Oh, my belly. It hurts. I have never felt such a pain. You shot me good, Senor."

"Why did you turn on us, Ortega?" Jim asked, calling from the dark.

Ortega took a few more wheezing, gasping breaths. Then the sound stopped.

"Ortega?"

There was no response. Slowly, Jim moved through the darkness toward the place from where he had heard Ortega's voice. When he got close enough, he could see the Mexican lying on his back. His pistol was on the ground beside him, and both hands were folded across his belly, as if trying to hold back the pain. His eyes were open, and though they reflected light from the moon, they had a glassy, lifeless look about them. Moving closer still, Jim nudged Ortega with this foot. Then he knelt beside him for a closer look.

Ortega was dead.

Chapter 19

It was evening of the following day before Jim reached civilization. The night creatures called out to each other as Jim stood looking toward the small Mexican village. A cloud passed over the moon, then moved away, bathing in silver the little town that rose up like a ghost before him. A couple of dozen adobe buildings, half of which were lit, fronted the town plaza. The biggest and most brightly lit building was the lone cantina at the far end of town.

Inside the cantina someone was playing a guitar, and Jim could hear the music all the way out in the hills. The guitarist was good, and the music spilled out a steady beat with two or three poignant minor chords at the end of each phrase. An overall, single-string melody worked its way in and out of the chords like a thread of gold woven through the finest cloth. Jim liked that kind of music. It was a mournful, lonesome music, the kind of melody a man could let run through his mind during long, lonely nights watching over a herd.

Jim was somewhat hesitant about riding into the village. Although his outfit badly needed beans, rice, bacon, salt, and coffee, he didn't want a repeat of what had happened to them at Escalon. On the other hand, if he didn't get some supplies soon, they would all starve before they got out of Mexico.

He checked his pistol. It was loaded and slipped easily from its sheath. Then, clucking at his horse, he began riding slowly toward the town, being especially alert as he rode in.

He heard a dog's bark, a ribbony yap that was silenced by a kick or a thrown rock. A baby cried, a sudden gargle that cracked through the air like a bullwhip. A housewife raised her voice in one of the houses. Even though Jim couldn't understand the language, he could understand the tone, as the woman shared her anger with all who were within earshot.

Jim stepped up onto the porch of the cantina, then pushed his way inside. Because he was the only American in the place, he drew instant attention. However, if anyone had any ideas toward causing him any trouble, they didn't show it. Instead, they gave him no more than a perfunctory glance, then returned to their own conversations. The conversations of two dozen men, speaking in Spanish, was a cacophony of undecipherable sound, though none of it seemed threatening.

"Do you have any whiskey?" he asked the bartender.

"No, senor. Tequila."

"All right. Tequila."

The bartender reached for a bottle and a glass, then poured the drink. He slid the glass across the bar to him.

"*Dos pesos, senor,*" he said, holding up two fingers.

Jim paid for his drink. "You speak English?" he asked.

"Sí, I speak English."

"Some pards and I are trailing a herd of horses back up to the States. We need some supplies: rice, beans, bacon, flour, coffee—that sort of thing. Is there a store in town where such things can be bought?"

"Sí, senor. But the store is closed now. It will open mañana."

"I'd like to get the stuff and start back tonight," Jim said. "Any chance the store owner will open tonight?"

"Sí, I think he will open tonight. But it will cost more money."

"Then I will wait until morning," Jim said. He tossed the drink down, then tapped the glass, indicating that he wanted another. The bartender filled it, took his money, then walked away to wait on another customer.

"Senor," a voice called.

When Jim looked toward the sound of the voice, he saw a boy of about twelve who was sweeping the floor behind him

"I can get the things you need for less money than you can get them in the store," the boy offered.

"How much less?"

"Much less. You will see," the boys aid.

"All of it? Beans, rice, bacon?"

"Sí," the boy answered after each item, nodding his head.

"Salt, pepper, coffee, flour?"

"Everything," the boy promised.

"When can I get it?"

"Tonight," the boy said. He looked around the cantina, as if to make certain he wasn't being overheard. "Are you hungry? I will show you where you can get a good meal. While you are eating, I will get the things you need."

"Where will you get them?"

"I know a place," the boy replied mysteriously. He leaned the broom against the wall. "Come with me. I will show you a good place where you can eat while you wait."

"I was just going to get something to eat in here," Jim said.

The boy shook his head. "No, you do not want to do that," he said. "The food here is not so good as it is at Mamacita's."

"Mamacita? Your mother?"

"Not my mamacita," the boy replied. "The café—it is called Mamacita's."

The idea of eating in a restaurant rather than in a cantina was very appealing to Jim.

"All right," he said. "Maybe I'll take you up on that. I'll eat my supper while you get the supplies I need and bring them to me."

"Come with me, senor."

From the moment Jim set foot inside the restaurant, he knew he had made the right decision. The aromas were so enticing that they made his stomach rumble. He felt the contrasting emotions of eager anticipation and a terrible sense of guilt. Here he was, about to enjoy a good meal, while those he had left behind were on their last strips of jerky.

A large, smiling woman greeted him. She was wearing an apron that was dusted with flour, chili powder, and perhaps half a dozen other spices and condiments.

"*Buenas noches*, senor," she said pleasantly.

The boy, who had said his name was Pancho, spoke to the woman and she nodded.

"I told her you do not speak Spanish," Pancho explained. "If you will tell me what you want, I will order for you."

"How about a steak, chili, and coffee?" Jim asked.

Pancho gave the order. Then as the woman headed for the kitchen, the boy told Jim he would go get his supplies now.

"Maybe you had better wait until I've had my supper. Then you can take me there," Jim suggested.

"No, senor, that will not be good," Pancho replied, shaking his head.

"Why not?"

"Because the man who owns the store will not sell to a gringo."

"I see. So you want me to trust you with the money—is that it?"

"Sí, senor."

"What if I give you the money and you skedaddle?"

"*Qué?*"

"Run away," Jim explained. "If I give you the money, how do I know I'll see you again?"

The boy shook his head ardently. "Senor, I will not run away," he said.

"It's easy for you to say that, Pancho, but I've never seen you before. I can't just turn my money over to you without some assurance that you will come back with the goods."

"You do not have to give me the money now. Give me the money when I bring the supplies to you."

"Are you telling me the storekeeper will let you have it without having to pay for it first?"

Pancho smiled. "Sí."

"Well, then you must be pretty trustworthy after all. All right, Pancho. If you can do that, gather up what I need, meet me back here, and I'll pay for it," Jim promised.

Nodding, Pancho left on his errand.

A few minutes later, the woman brought Jim's meal. It was as delicious as promised, and after he finished his supper, he asked for a plate of tamales, not because he was still hungry, but because the food was so good.

As the woman headed for the kitchen to fill Jim's order, Pancho opened the back door and came in, carrying two large cloth bags.

Jim smiled at him. "Good for you, Pancho. You did it."

"I think maybe you should pay me now," Pancho said.

"All right. How much was it?"

"One hundred pesos."

Jim whistled softly. "One hundred pesos? That's a little steep, isn't it? I thought you said you were going to be able to save me money."

"Fifty pesos," Pancho said.

"Whoa, now, that's quite a difference. So which is it? One hundred pesos or fifty pesos?"

"Will you pay one hundred pesos?" Pancho asked.

"No."

"Will you pay fifty pesos?"

"Yes."

Pancho smiled and nodded his head. "Then it is fifty pesos."

Jim took the money from his pocket and handed it to Pancho. "I have to tell you, Pancho, there is something a little fishy about this whole transaction."

"I brought your horse around back, senor," Pancho said. "I think maybe you should take your supplies and go now."

"What do you mean, go now?" Jim asked. "I just ordered a plate of tamales."

Even as he was explaining the situation to Pancho, a plate of steaming tamales was set on the table.

"I think you will not have time to eat your

tamales," Pancho said. Without being offered one, Pancho picked up one of the spicy cylinders of ground meat, slipped it from its corn husk wrapping, and began eating.

"Pancho, why must I leave now?"

"I think you will not want to be here when the storekeeper discovers some of his things are gone."

"What the hell? Pancho, did you steal these vittles?"

"Sí," Pancho said in a matter-of-fact voice. "It was easy," he added.

"Take it back," Jim said, holding the sacks toward him. "Take it all back."

At that moment, there was a loud commotion out on the plaza. A man was shouting, but because he was shouting in Spanish, Jim had no idea what he was saying.

"I think it is too late to take it back now," Pancho said, reaching for another tamale. "I think maybe you had better go quickly. Everyone heard you talk about getting supplies when you were in the cantina. Now when they see you with these things, they will think you are the thief."

Jim realized that Pancho was right. There was no way he could talk his way out of this, and even if he could, it would be at Pancho's expense.

On the other hand, he had more than an ample supply of the goods he needed, and he had gotten it at a bargain rate. And if his horse was behind the café as Pancho had promised, then it shouldn't be that difficult for him to get away.

"Is my horse really behind the café?" Jim asked.

"Sí, I brought him there myself. If you go quickly, you will get away before anyone else can get a horse."

"All right," Jim said, hefting the two bags. "I'll take your advice and get out of here." He started toward the back door, but just before he left, he turned toward the boy. "I'll give you this," he said. "You are an enterprising young man, Pancho . . . Pancho what? What is your last name?"

"Villa," the boy said with a broad smile. "My name is Pancho Villa."

Chapter 20

Jim Robison was a very welcome sight when he rode into camp carrying two large cloth bags filled with groceries.

"This is wonderful!" Katie said as she began taking inventory of the food Jim brought with him. "What did you do? Buy out the store? There's chili powder, cinnamon, onions, dried apples, dried peaches, raisins, cornmeal, molasses—all sorts of things."

Jim had no idea that young Pancho Villa had been so thorough in his "shopping." He hadn't even bothered to look into the sacks, so quickly had he left the little village.

"I thought a few extra things might be nice," he said.

"I'll show you just how nice it can be," Katie

said. "Girls, help me out here. No more beef jerky. Tonight, we eat well."

"Oh, Lord, Miz Katie," Frank said, rubbing his stomach after the meal that evening. "I know I said I wasn't ready to settle down with any one woman, but I swear if I could find one that cooks like this, I might be tempted."

Katie laughed. "Well, thank you, Frank. I'll take that as a compliment."

True to her promise, Katie and her daughters had prepared a veritable feast that evening. She had made a main course of beans, rice, onions, and bacon, liberally seasoned with chili powder. In addition to the main course, she had baked an apple pie and flavored it with cinnamon and molasses. The meal was washed down with copious amounts of coffee.

After paying homage to Katie and her daughters for preparing such a banquet, the four young men settled down with a final cup of coffee and a smoke. It was a time of contentment for all of them, and though Jim didn't put it into words, he realized that this was what he liked best about being a cowboy.

He knew that people who lived in town could also have a good meal, a cup of coffee, and a pipe or a cigarette. But he also knew that, without the hard life of a cowboy to isolate such moments, there was no way anyone could enjoy them nearly as much as he did.

"I've been giving this business about Ortega some considerable thought," Frank said as he used a burning brand to light his rolled cigarette. "What do you reckon he was really after?" Frank asked.

"He said he was after the women and the horses," Jim said.

"The women, yes—he could sell them just like Shardeen planned, I suppose," Frank said. "But what was he going to do with the horses?"

"I figure he was planning on delivering them to Allison, then collecting all the rest of the money himself," Barry said.

Frank shook his head. "I don't think so."

"Well, what do you think?" Barry asked.

"I think the son of a bitch was going to steal the horses. He didn't have no plans to take 'em back to Allison."

"What would he do with 'em, if he did steal 'em?" Gene asked.

"Sell 'em, I reckon," Frank replied.

"I wouldn't sell 'em if they were mine," Jim said.

"You wouldn't? What would you do with them?"

"If I had these horses, I'd get myself a little spread somewhere and keep 'em for about a year. That way, they'd have plenty of time to get adjusted to being tame. During the year, I'd breed as many of the stallions and mares as I could get together. Then come spring, I'd sell off about half as many horses as there had been new colts born, just to get enough money to keep the ranch running. Within a year or two, I'd have as good a horse ranch as you ever want to see."

"You got any idea where that ranch would be?" Barry asked.

"Not really."

" 'Cause from what Marilou has been telling me, the Kincaid Ranch would be just the place for something like that."

"Yeah," Gene added. "You could start running horses there, and me an' Barry could work for you."

"You're forgettin' a couple of things," Jim said. "In the first place, this isn't my herd to do with as I please. And in the second place, I don't have anything to do with the Kincaid Ranch."

"You could," Barry said.

"Yeah," Gene added. "You may not have noticed, but Miz Katie has her cap set for you."

Damn, Jim thought. *Has she made it that obvious to everyone?*

"And we could have these horses, too," Frank said.

Frank's comment was greeted with a moment of shocked silence.

"Are you suggesting we steal the horses?" Jim asked.

"I'm not sure I'd call it stealin'," Frank said. "If you stop an' think about it, we're the ones who had to break the horses. By rights, that should make 'em ours."

"Frank's got a point," Gene said.

"If we had rounded them up as well, perhaps he would have a point," Jim said. "But we didn't round them up. They were already gathered. All we had to do was break them. Besides, do you really want to take horses from someone like Clay Allison? He's not the kind of fella that I would want for an enemy."

"Me, neither," Barry said.

Frank took another puff, then blew out a long cloud of smoke. "I reckon, now that you mention it, I wouldn't want to cross him, either."

"You are probably right," Gene said. He was silent for a moment, then he smiled. "But it was grand thinking about it for a few minutes."

Capitán Eduardo Bustamante, Teniente Santos, and Sargento Gonzales were with a company of more than forty Federales, waiting for

the Americans. Their scouts had reported that
the Americans, with the women, were leading a
herd of horses north, and Bustamante knew they
would have to come right through here, a place
called Diablo Canyon, in order to reach the U.S.
border. Here, the trail squeezed down to a narrow pass, closed in on either side by sheer rock
cliffs. There were no exits from the pass. Once
the Americans were committed, they would
have no choice but to go on through. It was the
perfect place for an ambush.

Bustamante put Santos in command of the
men on the west side of the pass, while he took
command of the men on the east side. He had
already given the word not to fire until he gave
the signal. The agreed-upon signal would be
when he fired the first shot.

"It is a brilliant plan, Capitán," Gonzales said.
Gonzales was on the east side of the pass with
Bustamante.

"It is an example of what one can do with
organization and planning," Bustamante replied. "Unlike your disastrous operation in
Escalon."

"Sí, Capitán," Gonzales replied in chagrin. Although he had already been thoroughly repri-
manded for letting the Americans evade capture
in Escalon, Bustamante was not letting him live

it down. Indeed, he would not even be present now had he not begged to be included, reminding Bustamante that he was one of the few who could identify the Americans by sight.

"What about the women?" Gonzales asked, as they waited.

"What about the women?" Bustamante replied.

"The women are riding with the Americans. They might get hurt when we start shooting."

"They are not innocent victims. Our scouts tell us that the women are riding willingly," Bustamante said.

"Capitán, does it not concern you that the women are riding willingly?"

"Why should that concern me?"

"Does it not prove that they are not captives, as we once thought?"

"It doesn't matter whether they are captives or not," Bustamante replied. "I am no longer hunting these men for the American authorities. I hunt them now because they committed murder in Escalon."

"But if they are not the ones who captured the women, then they are not murderers in the fullest sense of the word. They are guilty only of defending themselves," Gonzales said. "For it was we who fired first."

Bustamante glared at Gonzales. "Sargento Gonzales, you lost many fine citizens in Escalon, including Reyna, your own diputado. Do you now say that you do not want revenge?"

"It troubles me that these may have been innocent men whom we fired upon by mistake. If so, they would have killed no one, had I not ordered my men to shoot at them. Perhaps the guilt is mine."

"Your only guilt is that you let them get away. Do not concern yourself that they may be innocent. They are the ones who killed Teniente Montoya and Teniente Arino, of that I am certain. When I give the signal to begin shooting, you will shoot as ordered. Am I understood, Sargento?"

"Sí," Gonzales replied.

"Capitán Bustamante, they are coming!" someone yelled.

Bustamante gave the signal for everyone to get down. Then he ducked behind a rock and jacked a shell into the chamber of his rifle. He thought of the funeral of his two lieutenants, and he remembered the promise he had made to their widows. His blood ran hot as he waited.

Jim had spotted Bustamante's scouts more than an hour earlier, and he surmised that an ambush may be awaiting them when they reached Diablo Canyon.

"I'm not going to mince words with you," he told the others, once he figured out what lay ahead. "The way I see it, we have only two choices. We can either try and force our way through, maybe by blending in with the herd and hoping that gives us some protection, or we can just abandon the horses and hightail it out of here, finding some other way back home."

"Damn, I hate to give up the herd now, after all we've been through," Frank said. "I'm for trying to force our way through."

"I don't see how we can do it without a couple of us getting killed," Barry said.

"I'm willing to take that chance," Frank replied.

"What about the women? Are you willing to take the chance with their lives? They don't have any stake in this. They were brought down here against their will," Gene said.

"They don't have to go through with us," Frank said. "They can leave now and find some other way back. And if we are keeping whoever is waiting for us at the canyon busy, that will give them a better chance."

"None of us have to go through the canyon," Katie suggested. "There is another way through."

"Another way?"

"Yes. It's called Purgatory's Needle. That's the way Shardeen brought us through when we came south," Katie said. "I paid close attention to it, because I figured on getting away somehow, and I thought I might need to know."

"How far away is the other way?" Jim asked.

"Not far at all. Only about a quarter of a mile west of the canyon opening."

"Wait a minute. Are you telling me there are two canyons running parallel to each other?"

"Well, Purgatory's Needle isn't exactly a canyon," Katie explained. "It's more like a very narrow chute. But if we ride single file, we can get through it."

"What about the herd?" Gene asked.

Katie shook her head. "There's no way the horses can get through there."

"Then we are back where we started," Gene complained.

"Maybe not," Jim said. "I have an idea."

Jim's idea was to start through the needle with the three women, Gene, and Barry. Frank, who was arguably the best rider of the entire outfit, would remain behind. His job was to start the herd through Diablo Canyon. By firing a couple of shots behind the horses, Frank would start them running through the canyon.

Jim believed that the horses would draw fire from whoever was waiting for them, and that shooting would urge the horses on, thus ensuring that they ran all the way through the canyon. It would also keep the bushwhackers occupied so that they might not notice the absence of Jim and the others.

When Jim, Gene, Barry, Katie, and her daughters were in position at the mouth of Purgatory's Needle, Frank fired three shots, and the canyon echoed them back, giving the illusion of many more shots being fired. The horses, just as Jim hoped they would, broke into a frenzied gallop.

As the horses rushed through the canyon, the discipline Bustamante had counted on from his men broke. One man fired, then the others, thinking that was the signal from Bustamante, began firing as well. Scores of shots rang out, echoing loudly through the canyon walls. Panic-stricken, the horses ran faster.

"Where are they?" Busamante shouted, looking down at the galloping horses, trying to find the Americans. "Where are they?"

"I don't know," Gonzales shouted. "I don't see anyone!"

"Stop firing! Stop firing!" Bustamante shouted, standing up and waving his arms.

Bustamante's attempt to stop the shooting

went unheeded. The shooting continued until the last horse thundered through to the other side of the canyon. Behind, five horses lay dead, two from bullet wounds, and three from broken necks brought about by collision during the melee.

"There they are!" Gonzales shouted, pointing to the north. There, nearly a mile ahead, Bustamante saw the Americans rejoining the horses, their stampede now over.

"Get them!" he shouted. "Get them!"

"Capitán, they are nearly to the border," Gonzales said. "Even if we were mounted, we wouldn't be able to catch up with them."

Bustamante stood on the edge of the cliff and cursed in impotent frustration. Gonzales turned from Bustamante, so his *capitán* wouldn't see the smile on his face. He wasn't the only one who had let the Americans get away.

They didn't need a sign telling them they had returned to the United States. They crossed a river, and though it was much the same as rivers they had crossed over the last several days, once they were on the other side, the difference was palpable.

Texas.

It was home because of language, though in

this part of Texas nearly as many people spoke Spanish as spoke English. It was home because of the attitude, because here no man would ever let another assume authority over him by reason of birth, position, or wealth.

"I say there," Jim once heard an Englishman say to a cowboy. "Could you direct me to your superior?"

The cowboy spit a wad of tobacco at the Englishman's feet, then glared at him. "Mister, that son of a bitch hasn't been born yet," he said.

Jim left the herd just outside El Paso while he went into town to send a telegram to Clay Allison. That was when he learned that Allison was dead. He hurried back to the others to share the news.

Frank smiled. "Then that settles it," he said. "We take the horses to the Kincaid Ranch."

"What about it, Jim? Do we?" Gene asked. Marilou stepped up next to Gene, while Brenda sidled up to Barry. Gene, Barry, and both girls looked at Jim, the expressions on their faces indicating the answer they wanted to hear from him.

"I reckon something like that would be up to Katie," Jim finally said.

"I can't think of any better way to start a new life," Katie said.

Jim smiled broadly. "All right, boys, let's get this herd out to the ranch."

It was just after dusk by the time they turned the herd onto the Kincaid rangeland. With the horses finally delivered, and their long journey over, everyone was looking forward to a home-cooked supper, then a good night's rest. What none of them realized was that Shardeen was waiting for them in the barn.

Shardeen had correctly figured that, once they got word of Allison's death, they would bring the horses here, to the Kincaid Ranch. He had watched them turn the horses out into the pasture. Then he hurried back to set up his surprise for them.

"Are they comin'?" Tom Dingus asked. Shardeen had picked up Dingus and three other men in town. He had made the mistake last time of trying to take the Robison outfit on with just two men, believing that position and surprise would carry the day for him. This time he had five guns, plus position and surprise. He was taking absolutely no chances.

"Dingus, take Pete with you and get over there by the granary shed. That way, we'll have them in a cross fire. Open up on them as soon as they get into range," Shardeen said.

"Come on, Pete," Dingus said, starting from the barn toward the granary shed. He turned back toward Shardeen. "What about the women?" he asked.

"What about 'em?"

"They're likely to get caught up in the line of fire."

"Don't matter none to me. Kill the women, too," Shardeen said. "I want 'em all dead."

As Jim and the others approached the ranch, they were in high spirits. They were totally unprepared for what happened next.

A gunshot rang out from the dark maw of the barn. That shot was followed by another and another until soon the entire valley rang with the crash and clatter of rifle and pistol fire. Gun flashes lit up the night, and bullets whistled and whined by the returning cowboys.

"Who's shooting at us?" Gene shouted.

"Katie, take the girls and get out of here!" Jim shouted. "Gene, you and Barry go right. Frank, come left with me!"

As the guns banged and crashed around them, the four men split up, two running to the right and two going to the left, in order to get out of the line of fire. As they did, Jim made plans as to how he could get to the barn.

"Look there. Maybe we can use that," Jim said, pointing. "Looks like that gully winds around all the way up to the barn."

The shooting continued unabated, and Jim noticed with some surprise that their assailants seemed to be shooting at each other. Almost as soon as Jim made the discovery, Dingus and Pete came to the same conclusion. After much shouting and calling, the shooting finally stopped.

"You dumb bastards! You were shooting at us!" Dingus called.

"Well, what the hell were you doing in the way?" Shardeen called back through the night.

"I'm here because you told me to be here!" Dingus answered.

Taking advantage of the confusion, Jim made his move. Running low and crouching over, he darted through the darkness until he reached the edge of the barn. Then he slipped inside.

"Where'd they go?" Jim heard Shardeen ask. The voice was close, no more than fifteen feet away. Jim stood very still and looked toward the sound of the voice. He was rewarded for his patience when Shardeen stepped out of the shadows and into the doorway. That had the effect of silhouetting him against the lighter area outside the barn.

"I'm right here," Jim said from within the barn.

"Son of a bitch!" Shardeen shouted, spinning around and firing. Even though Shardeen was only firing at the sound of his voice, his bullet came frighteningly close, so close that Jim felt the puff of air as the bullet sped past his head. Jim returned fire.

Shardeen went down.

"Shardeen!" one of his men called. He made the mistake of stepping out of the darkness so that he, too, was in silhouette.

"Mister, you just made the same mistake Shardeen did," Jim said. "I can see you clearly. Drop your gun."

"I'm dropping it. I'm dropping it," the man said.

"If anyone else is left in here, you'd better call him out," Jim said.

"There ain't no one else in here."

Jim cocked his pistol. "That lie just cost you your life," he said.

"No, wait! Wait! Arnie, come on out," the man called.

Arnie didn't move.

"Arnie, for God's sake, come on out!"

There was a scuffing sound. Then Arnie appeared in the door as well. He dropped his gun.

"What's your name?" Jim asked.

"Lester."

"Who is outside, Lester?"

"Dingus and Pete."

Jim moved to the edge of the door, but still didn't show himself.

"Dingus, Pete," he called.

"What do you want?"

"Lester and Arnie have given up. Shardeen is dead. You want to keep this up? You'll probably get killed, and even if you don't, there's nothing in it for you anymore."

There was a moment of silence. Then a voice answered, "No, don't shoot. We're comin' in."

Jim waited until he could see Dingus and Pete. Then he called out to them. "Drop your guns right there," he said.

Both men did as ordered. Then, holding their hands up, they came on up to the barn. By the time they reached the barn, Barry, Gene, Frank, Katie, Marilou, and Brenda had materialized out of the darkness.

"What are you going to do with us?" Dingus asked.

Jim studied each man's face for a long moment. "I'm going to kill you on sight if you ever show up on this ranch again," he said. "My advice to you is to get as far away from here as you can."

"That's fine with me," Dingus said. "I've always had a hankerin' to see California anyway."

"Good choice," Jim said.

"Come on, boys. Let's get out of here," Dingus said.

Lester started to pick up his gun.

"Leave your guns here," Jim ordered.

By now, Gene and Barry had led their horses over to them. Gene nodded toward Shardeen's body. "Take your trash with you," he said.

Nodding in assent, Lester and Arnie picked Shardeen up and threw him belly down across his horse. Then the outlaws mounted and rode away, disappearing into the darkness.

"I think maybe I'll follow along behind those fellas for a while, just to make certain they don't change their minds," Frank said.

"Good idea," Jim said.

"Barry, Gene, why don't you two come with Brenda and me?" Marilou said. "We'll show you the bunkhouse where you can stay."

Smiling, the cowboys followed the two young girls off into the dark. Now only Jim and Katie remained.

"I owe you so much," Katie said when they were alone.

"You don't owe me anything," Jim replied.

"Yes, I do," Katie insisted. "But what I owe you can't be paid with money."

Katie ringed Jim's neck with her arms, then kissed him hard on the lips.

"But if you are willing to negotiate, I think I can find some way to say thanks."

"I'm more than willing to negotiate," Jim said huskily, eagerly returning her kiss.